KU-631-321

DANCE CLUB

1

FOOTPRINT IN THE CLAY

•

Mal Lewis Jones

MACDONALD YOUNG BOOKS

Text copyright © Mal Lewis Jones 1996

First published in Great Britain in 1996
by Macdonald Young Books
61 Western Road
Hove
East Sussex
BN3 1JD

All rights reserved.
This book is sold subject to the condition that it shall not, by way of trade
or otherwise, be lent, re-sold, hired out, or otherwise circulated without
the publisher's prior consent in any form of binding or cover other than
that in which it is published and without a similar condition including this
condition being imposed on the subsequent purchaser.

The right of Mal Lewis Jones to be identified as author of this work has
been asserted by her in accordance with the Copyright, Designs and
Patents Act 1988.

All characters in this publication are fictitious and any resemblance to real
persons, living or dead, is purely coincidental.

Photoset in North Wales by
Derek Doyle & Associates, Mold, Clwyd.
Printed and bound in Great Britain by
The Guernsey Press Co. Ltd.

British Library Cataloguing in Publication Data available.

ISBN: 0 7500 1959 X
ISBN: 0 7500 2133 0 (pb)

Contents

First Day at Bishop's School

Annie's knees trembled slightly as she waved goodbye to her mother and walked through the gates of her new school. The Bishop's School was an imposing Victorian red-brick building poised on one bank of the River Severn.

But it wasn't the building that made her nervous. It was the children. Milling about everywhere, shouting and laughing. English children, not Scots like her. In the north of Scotland, she was a Macdonald. Here, she was a nobody.

She bit her lip and made up her mind to approach the first girl of around her own age that she came across in the yard. She wasn't used to feeling nervous; at her old secondary school, she had been popular and confident, even though she was only in her first year. Then came the bombshell. Her parents wanted to move to Shrewsbury; a good career move for her dad.

Now here she was, at the beginning of Year 8, a stranger in a new and totally different school and environment.

A girl with a mane of reddish-gold, wavy hair caught her eye. Though she was quite tall, Annie thought she looked about twelve. Determined to overcome her feelings of nervousness, she crossed the yard towards the girl.

'Hello, I'm new around here!' she shouted. 'Could you give me a few clues about finding my way around, sorta thing?'

The red-headed girl smiled at her. She had a pale, freckly face, which lit up when she smiled. And her green eyes were full of laughter.

'Hi. Thought I hadn't seen you before. I'm Cherry Stevens.'

'Annie Macdonald.'

'Hi again,' giggled Cherry. 'Hey, you're not from round here are you? You haven't got a Shropshire accent. Where is it you're from? Ireland?'

'Nay,' laughed Annie, 'north of Scotland.'

Two of the older lads jostled into them. One was about six foot tall, the other much shorter, and slightly built.

'Na-a-a-ay,' repeated the smaller one. 'That's what horses do!'

2

Annie felt a stab of fear.

The boys laughed uproariously, slapping each other on the back and pretending to fall over.

Annie's face flushed red. She felt her temper rising. Her sapphire eyes flashed dangerously, as she tossed her dark hair over her shoulder.

'Baaa would be nearer the mark for you two!'

The boys stopped short and looked at her open-mouthed, amazed that she'd had the guts to answer them back. As Cherry started giggling, the shorter boy stepped forward.

'Watch it!' he hissed, waving his finger in front of Annie's nose, before walking off with his sidekick.

'Who was that?' Annie burst out.

'Darren Charles and the big one was Wayne Doe,' Cherry replied.

'Are all the laddies like those two?' asked Annie. Her anger had subsided, leaving her with the sickly taste of fear, and a weak feeling in her legs.

'Not really,' said Cherry. 'They're the worst at Bishop's, by far. The funny thing is, they always manage to stay out of trouble in the classroom. But they're awful to the younger ones in the school.'

Annie inwardly breathed a sigh of relief. If she'd met the worst, then everyone else she encountered must be better! She always tried to look on the bright side. She was missing Scotland, her old home, her schoolmates and her dancing friends. But that was no reason to be glum. She was determined to make more friends and a new and interesting life for herself in Shrewsbury.

'So what year are you in?' Cherry asked her.

'Eight,' Annie replied. 'And I'm supposed to be in Mrs Clanger's form. I dinna, I mean, I *don't* know where that is, though.'

Cherry was grinning at her. 'Well, you're in luck, 'cause I'm in her form too – 8C. Come on, I'll show you the formroom.'

Annie happily followed her through a maze of corridors and into a smallish, high-windowed classroom.

'This is it!' said Cherry, perching herself on the teacher's desk.

'I'm lost already,' laughed Annie. 'This place is like a rabbit-warren.'

'Don't worry,' said Cherry. 'I'll steer you around. It's a pretty friendly school. So, what kind of things do you like doing?'

'Well,' replied Annie. 'Dancing's my main hobby. And it doesn't leave me much time for anything else – once homework's out of the way.'

'Dancing!' Cherry shrieked. 'It's my hobby too!'

The two girls gazed at each other in the otherwise empty classroom, their eyes wide with surprise.

'This is amazing!' Annie cried. 'What lessons do you take?'

'Ballet, Modern and tap. But I like Modern and tap best. How about you?'

'Aye. I do all three too, but ballet and National are my favourites.'

'You sound really keen,' said Cherry. 'My dance

teacher does all those classes, if you want to do them.'

'That's great!' cried Annie. 'What's her name?'

'Miss Rodelle,' answered Cherry. 'She's only been in Shrewsbury just over a year.'

'Is she nice?' asked Annie. 'My old teacher was lovely.'

'Yes, very nice. She's quite young and really enthusiastic. Hasn't been teaching all that long. But you have to work hard for her – she won't let you get away with sloppy work.'

'I still can't believe I've already found someone who's dance-mad like me!' Annie exclaimed. 'But have you only been going to dancing lessons for a year?'

Annie thought to herself that eleven was rather a late start. She herself had started Pre-primary ballet class at the age of three-and-a-half!

'Oh no,' giggled Cherry. 'I started ages ago. I went to the Wenlock Theatre School first. That's in the middle of town, but I didn't like the teachers much, so when I saw Miss Rodelle's advert, I moved to her.'

Annie frowned. 'I think Mum's booked me into the Wenlock school. I'm supposed to be starting next week.'

'Miss Rodelle's much nicer,' said Cherry. 'The Wenlock Principal has her favourites. And I wasn't one of them!'

The girls had been so intent on chatting that they hadn't noticed the school bell. Soon after, the other

5

children in their form started coming into the room, in twos and threes and Cherry had to show Annie the cloakroom and locker area. When they came back, everyone else was already seated, and the form tutor, Mrs Clanger, was taking the register. She broke off to welcome Annie and give her a big smile.

'You don't have to be mad to be in this class, but it helps!' Mrs Clanger announced.

The class laughed dutifully. They were used to Mrs Clanger's 'little jokes'.

Annie liked her immediately. She had a little, perky face, with enormous glasses and a halo of frizzed-out hair.

'She teaches us English,' Cherry whispered. 'She's ever so funny. The other Year 8s have got boring form tutors. We're really lucky.'

Annie thanked her lucky stars. Everything was turning out fine.

After register, there was a short time for form matters to be sorted out, and any problems aired. Then, a girl sitting at the side put her hand up and started asking Mrs Clanger about choir practice. The girl was attractive, beautiful even, thought Annie. She had a rich tan and her glossy black hair hung in a long plait down her back. Her eyes were such a dark brown they were almost black and she had similarly dark, dramatic eyebrows. A straight nose and a wide full mouth completed the pleasing picture.

'My violin lesson has been booked for the same lunch-hour,' the girl was saying.

'Oh that's a bit much,' Mrs Clanger replied,

6

light-heartedly. 'You're going to get over-musicked on Thursdays!'

The girl didn't smile. Her eyes didn't even flicker. 'It is very important,' she said, 'that I do not miss *any* choir-practice. I think you'll agree.'

The tone in which she said this seemed to give Mrs Clanger no option *but* to agree,

'I'll look into it, Maria,' the form-teacher said, this time seriously.

'That's Maria Farran,' whispered Cherry. 'She's half-Spanish.'

'I thought she looked rather exotic. What's she like?' asked Annie.

'Fine if you stay on the right side of her,' said Cherry. 'So be warned. She goes to the Wenlock dancing school by the way.'

Annie made a mental note to have a chat to Maria Farran some time during the day. But first, as they moved out of the classroom to go to their first lesson, she was introduced to one of Cherry's friends.

'This is Pip Williams,' said Cherry, with a giggle. 'She comes to Miss Rodelle's classes too.'

Annie allowed herself to be jostled along in the group, down the corridor, as Cherry chatted to Pip.

Pip had very fine, bobbed blonde hair, which fell like curtains from a middle parting, hiding half of her round face. Her eyes were the lightest blue you could imagine and slanted downwards slightly.

The general impression Annie got was one of untidiness – Pip's uniform looked crumpled and slightly askew.

7

'Where have you moved from?' Pip asked her.

'North-east of Scotland. We used to live in a little fishing village on the coast.'

'That sounds lovely,' said Cherry. 'Are you missing it?'

'Aye,' Annie answered. 'I do. But it's warmer down here, you ken.'

'Ken?' said Cherry, looking round.

'Who's he?' asked Pip.

Annie laughed. '*You ken* just means *you know*!'

'Oh!' chorused Pip and Cherry.

'Is that why you moved?' asked Pip.

'No,' Annie replied. 'My dad was offered a job on a bigger newspaper down here – the *Shropshire Star*. He's a journalist.' She was proud of him and it showed in her voice.

'You're dead lucky,' Cherry sighed, 'having a dad with an exciting job like that.'

This made Annie curious to know what Cherry's parents did; but she was prevented from asking her by a slim, dark-haired boy, who had planted himself in her path. Taken by surprise, Annie was reassured by his wide, friendly grin.

'Hi!' he said, holding out his hand. 'Annie, isn't it? I'm Sam Murray.'

'Pleased to meet you,' Annie said, warming straight away to the friendliness of his manner.

'Well, I just wanted to say, hope you settle in OK,' said Sam, tossing his longish black hair out of his eyes. 'Any problems, you come and see me.'

'Well thank you,' said Annie, 'but I'm getting

8

along just fine. Pip and Cherry here are looking after me.'

Sam's expression changed instantly, 'Right,' he said gruffly and walked off without a glance at either Pip or Cherry.

'Did I say something?' asked Annie in stonishment.

Pip shrugged. 'Oh, don't take any notice. He's not speaking to either of us, that's all.'

'He goes to the Wenlock Theatre School, you see,' said Cherry, as if that explained everything.

'Maria and Sam have both stopped speaking to us since we left to go to Miss Rodelle,' Pip added. 'They think we're sort of traitors!'

They reached the geography room at this point in the conversation and Annie was left to ponder upon their remarks during the double lesson.

At break-time, Cherry had to run an errand for the geography teacher, while Pip rushed off to the cloakrooms to attempt to read a book which she was supposed to have read during the holiday.

For the first time since entering the school gates that morning, Annie was left to her own devices. She perched herself on a low wall at one side of the yard, watching the hundreds of youngsters scurrying to and fro, like bees. Their uniform of brown and yellow aided this impression. She suddenly felt small and insignificant, alone in the middle of all this group activity.

'On your own?' said a voice behind her. Annie jumped and looked round.

It was Maria Farran and another girl from her class. Maria introduced herself and her friend, Zoë, who was as plain as Maria was striking.

'You look like a dancer,' said Maria, knowingly.

'Aye, I am,' said Annie in surprise. 'And you too, I've been hearing.'

'Oh?' said Maria, with a questioning look.

'I've been wanting to talk to you,' said Annie, 'to ask you about your dancing classes. I may be starting at the Wenlock Theatre School.'

Maria smiled encouragingly. 'Oh, that'll be *lovely*, won't it, Zoë? I know you'll enjoy it there. Of course, I'm in the Major classes now, which keep me pretty busy, but Zoë will be able to keep an eye on you.'

'Well,' said Annie, hesitating. 'I'm not absolutely sure I'm joining yet.'

'Oh you *must*,' said Maria persuasively. 'Mustn't she, Zoë? You'll just love it at Wenlock. Miss Vane was a *brilliant* dancer when she was young and she's such a good teacher.'

'Who's Miss Vane?' asked Annie.

'Our Principal,' Maria replied. 'But all the teachers are good – they expect a high standard and won't put up with any old rubbish.'

'Not like Miss Rodelle!' said Zoë with a snort.

Annie felt uneasy. 'It's quite a big school then?' she asked.

'Oh yes,' said Maria, 'and it's been going for ages. Of course, *you* might find it a stretch at first. You know, coming from up north. Wenlock's a top school – we do well in all the competitions and festivals. At national level as well.'

'I've never done any competition work,' Annie admitted.

'Oh, you'll *love* it. Won't she, Zoë?'

'It's great,' agreed Zoë. 'Especially when you win a medal or something.'

'So what grade are you in ballet?' asked Maria.

'Oh, I've finished my grades,' said Annie proudly. 'I passed my Grade Five last year.'

Was it her imagination, or did Annie see a sudden, if fleeting, sharpening of Maria's dark eyes?

'In a Major class like me then?' she said. 'How wonderful! Isn't that wonderful, Zoë? I had no idea! What about Modern?'

'Same standard,' Annie replied.

'Great,' said Maria, rather flatly this time. 'You'll be in my class then.'

The bell went and they all rushed off to the English room, ready for the next lesson.

'Don't forget,' called Maria across the classroom, before the teacher arrived. 'Wenlock is best!'

Annie saw Pip and Cherry exchange looks. She felt herself flushing, even though she knew she had nothing to feel guilty about. She seemed to have landed herself in a rather awkward situation.

Her mind was in a whirl. Dancing was very important to her. For as long as she could remember, she had wanted to be a dancer. Thus the choice of a good dancing teacher was very important. She had been lucky to find an excellent teacher in Aberdeen and luckier still that her

11

parents had been willing to ferry her back and forth for lessons.

Now she was settling into her new home and new school, dancing classes were the next thing to consider. But how was she going to choose between Miss Rodelle's and the Wenlock Theatre School? Whichever choice she made, she was going to make enemies by the look of it. In her first week!

She liked Cherry and Pip very much and wanted to stay friends with them. They had made Miss Rodelle sound much nicer than Miss Vane. But there again, Sam, Maria and Zoë had gone out of their way to be friendly to her. Their school was much more established. Maria had called it a 'top school', and she was obviously quite an advanced student herself. Also, the competition work sounded great – Annie had never before had the opportunity to test herself against students from other schools.

Oh, it was impossible. She seemed to have walked right into the middle of a feud between members of the two local dancing schools. However would she be able to choose between them?

· 2 ·

A Big Decision

Annie took the problem home with her. Home was no longer a white-washed fisherman's cottage, overlooking the harbour. Now it was a modern brick house on a small development on the outskirts of Shrewsbury.

'How was it?' asked her mum, as Annie dumped her school bag on the kitchen floor. 'And don't forget – your bag doesn't stay in here!'

'Nay bad, nay bad,' Annie answered in a rather tired voice. She sank down on a kitchen chair.

Her mother wiped her floury hands – she was preparing vegetable pasties for dinner – and made a cup of tea for them both. Annie thought she could see a few new lines on her mother's roundish face since they'd moved. Even so, she didn't look forty-five; there was only the tiniest hint of grey at her temples – the rest of her hair was still a lovely rich dark brown, like Annie's own.

'How was your day, Mum?' Annie asked.

'Fine. Just fine.' Mrs Macdonald sat down across the table from her daughter. 'I'm feeling quite settled in now at the building society. They've made me very welcome. How about Bishop's School?'

'Aye,' said Annie, 'everyone's been really nice.' Her mind flitted back to the two big lads who had taunted her. 'Well, almost everyone.'

'You look as if something's bothering you.'

Annie was always amazed how her mum could guess what was going on in her mind. She started to tell her about the hard choice she was faced with, regarding dancing classes. In the middle of the conversation, her younger sister, Louisa, burst into the room.

'Hi, you guys!' she yelled. 'What's for tea?'

Her mother laughed. 'Where does the "guys" bit come from?'

Louisa shrugged.

'It's probably from someone she's met at school,' said Annie. 'What's your new school like, anyway?'

Louisa had started at the local primary school that day. 'It's great!' she cried. 'The dinners were *lovely*. And they've got the cutest gerbils in our class.'

Grabbing a biscuit, Louisa flew out of the back door.

'She seems happy enough!' said Annie.

'Aye, I think we have one satisfied customer, at least,' said Mrs Macdonald. 'But, going back to your problem, Annie, I think you should go and see both schools for yourself. That's the only way to judge.'

Within the hour, Mrs Macdonald had telephoned Miss Vane and explained that Annie wanted a trial lesson before committing herself to starting at the Wenlock school, and had made a similar arrangement with Miss Rodelle.

She and Annie were careful not to discuss it at dinner, when Annie's father was home. Although he took an interest in the arts, Mr Macdonald tended to dismiss dancing as a waste of time, apart from Scottish dancing. He felt Annie spent far too much of her time going to dancing lessons and practising. Ambitious for his daughter to do well at school, he wouldn't appreciate the importance to her of choosing the right dancing teacher.

He had been frustrated in his own career by a lack of higher education, and he wasn't keen to let the same thing happen to Annie. Mr Macdonald was in all respects but this one, the kindest of fathers. Where dancing was concerned however, Annie knew she had to rely on her mum, and her mum alone.

Over the next few days school brought no help in coming to a decision. Annie felt she had to walk a tightrope between the two groups of friends, being careful not to fall on one side or the other. She warmed to Cherry more and more. Cherry was always so good-humoured and giggly, not really taking anything very seriously. She was delighted when Annie told her she was coming to Miss Rodelle's for a trial lesson.

'Oh I do hope you like her,' she said. 'It would be great for us to be together.'

Annie had discovered that Cherry, too, was at the same standard, and they would be in the same class. This surprised her at first, as Cherry didn't strike her as being particularly dedicated to her dancing, and confessed to doing very little practice between lessons.

But then Annie saw her new friend in action in the gym, and on the sports field. Cherry was a natural athlete.

'How did you get to be so sporty?' Annie asked her at the end of one school day, when they were changing out of their games kit.

'I don't know really,' said Cherry. 'It just happened. But I guess I saw my brothers doing amazing things when I was small, and I just wanted to copy them.'

'Have they got red hair too?'

'Just like me,' laughed Cherry.

'Are they much older than you?' asked Annie.

'Yes, quite a bit. They're both away at university now, so I only see them in the holidays. I miss them – it's so quiet at the Vicarage without them.'

'Is it strange, your dad being a vicar?' asked

Annie, curiously.

Cherry giggled. 'A bit. For a start, you never know who you're going to bump into in our house.'

'A vicarage sounds sort of romantic,' said Annie. 'Not like a modern box at Bayston Hill!'

'Well, at least you've got a good central heating system,' said Cherry. 'Our house is *freezing* in the winter. Look, why don't you come round this evening and see for yourself?'

Annie would have dearly liked to say yes, but couldn't. 'Nay, I'm sorry, Cherry. I have to go to the Wenlock School tonight for my trial lesson.'

Cherry's face faded. 'Oh I didn't realize.'

To make matters worse, Maria and Zoë stopped by, on their way out of the changing room.

'See you tonight!' Maria said to Annie.

'Oh – er – yes,' said Annie, feeling her cheeks flushing a little.

Maria glanced at Cherry, as she spoke to Annie. 'I just know you're going to love it at Wenlock. Come about ten minutes early, and I'll introduce you to everyone.'

'Thanks,' said Annie, 'I will.'

Cherry murmured a quick goodbye and went off before Annie had a chance to try and make amends. Sighing, she gathered her things together, before making a dash to catch her bus home.

Her mum dropped her off in the town centre at twenty-past six, at the entrance to the passageway leading to the school. Annie walked down the alley between the leaning walls and overhanging

17

windows of old Tudor houses.

Shrewsbury was full of alley-ways like this, and Annie still found them fascinating. This particular one – Coffee House Passage – led alongside the Music Hall.

Coffee House Passage opened out into a little courtyard, at the end of which a sign for WENLOCK THEATRE SCHOOL left her in no doubt she had reached her destination. It was the finest building in the alley, half-timbered and painted black and white.

Annie thought what a wonderful place for a dancing school, before she entered through the heavy, but low, oak front door. A corridor led her to the sound of rhythmical music and tapping feet. A tap class was obviously in progress in the studio.

She ventured upstairs, where she could hear voices, and found her way to the waiting-room. Maria was on the look-out for her luckily, and led her to the girls' changing room.

As she donned her own navy leotard, Annie was pleased to find that she was wearing the same colour as Maria and the other girls in the Pre-elementary class.

'Do you take the RAD exams here?' she asked.

'Yes,' said Maria. 'I always do well in exams, do you? Not like Zoë. Exams aren't your strong point are they, Zoë?'

Zoë grimaced. 'We can't all be as brilliant as you, Maria.'

The girls took her round the room, introducing

all the other students. Two of the faces looked very familiar. They were twins that Annie thought she had seen in the yard at Bishop's school.

'Kim and Susie Dorricott,' said Maria. 'They're in Year 7 at school. They join us for the Major work, though they haven't taken their Grade Five yet.'

'Hi, Annie!' they chorused, in the same high-pitched voices.

'Pleased to meet you,' said Annie. She tried not to stare too hard at them, but she was keen to try to tell them apart.

They both had long, fair, bushy hair, at this moment tidied back into buns, brown eyes and very long dark lashes. They gazed back at her, with their pretty, identical faces. She could not detect any difference between them at all.

By the time they made their way downstairs to the studio a little later, Annie already felt less of a stranger. Even so, as she went through her barre work, she was conscious of many pairs of eyes upon her — Maria's most of all. Annie felt very out of practice.

Miss Vane took the Major classes in ballet. Annie thought she looked forbidding. She had completely white hair and had an old-fashioned, rather odd style of dressing. It looked, Annie thought, as if she'd grabbed the first items in her wardrobe that came to hand. Her battered, white teaching shoes bulged with bunions.

Quite quickly, Annie became aware of how critical a teacher she was. The Principal stopped the class constantly, to pick them up on tiny faults. On several of these occasions, she gave them a short lecture on how they could never hope to get into a ballet company if such faults weren't corrected. And she told them little tales about her own experiences as a professional dancer, of which she was obviously very proud.

Annie found the anecdotes interesting, but wondered if they would get boring if she heard them every week.

As the lesson went on, Miss Vane grew more irritable. By the time the class were doing the jumping steps, she was positively foul-tempered.

'These entrechats are much too wild!' she exclaimed. 'Tight little beats. That's what I want to see. What I'm seeing now is *disgusting*. Once more! And! ...'

But before two further entrechats had been executed, she had stopped them once more. 'No, no!' she cried, pouncing forward like some little white bird about to peck a worm. She came to rest inches in front of Sam Murray's hot face.

'These just aren't *good* enough for this standard. Let me see you on your own.'

Annie felt for Sam as he went through the entrechat exercise once more. He jumped higher than anyone else in the room – and he wasn't the only boy – but he was failing to achieve the crispness needed.

I could help him, Annie thought to herself. She had struggled with her own entrechats for months, and knew just how to put him right.

Miss Vane threw up her hands. 'You must practise. All of you. More practice! Just watch Maria. She has the right idea.'

Annie and the others fell back and watched Maria do the exercise effortlessly.

'She can't do any wrong for Miss Vane,' Sam whispered in her ear.

After their curtseys and bows, the class was dismissed. Annie caught up with Sam before he disappeared into the boys' room.

'Bad luck,' she said kindly.

He grinned at her. 'Oh, she's always like that! I don't let it bother me. She gets the results from us. That's the main thing.'

'I suppose so,' said Annie.

'Miss Vane says dancers have to be tough. You need to grow a thick skin in this game. You soon get used to it, believe me.'

Annie could see Sam was sincere. She went off to the girls' changing room, wondering how long it would take her to get used to Miss Vane.

Maria and Zoë made a great fuss of her, and told her all about the last school show, and their parts in it. Then Maria described in great detail the solos she had performed in a recent dance festival, and even took her into the wardrobe room to show her the costumes she had worn. Annie was impressed.

There was a lot that attracted her to the Wenlock Theatre School. It was busy, successful and well-established. But she was not sure about Miss

Vane. Still, she would only have her for ballet class; she hadn't yet met the teachers for tap, Modern or National. It was so hard to judge after only one lesson!

During the next week at school, Cherry carefully avoided asking her about her lesson with Miss Vane. In fact, she steered away from the subject of dancing entirely. Annie felt a certain coolness had grown between them, and racked her brains to think of a way of regaining Cherry's easy-going friendship.

The problem was, they were always in larger groups. Though Cherry had been careful to support Annie in her first few days at Bishop's, now she turned once more to her other friends.

It wasn't until the actual day of her second trial lesson, that Annie managed to remind Cherry that she was coming to Miss Rodelle's that evening.

'I'd forgotten,' said Cherry, but Annie knew as she said it that she hadn't. She sensed Cherry's feelings had been hurt.

'Um, you know last week, you asked me round to your place,' Annie said, 'Well, I'm not sure of the way to the school and I wondered if I could come round to your house first?'

Cherry looked first surprised and then pleased. 'Oh, I didn't think ... Yes, of course you can!'

'That's settled then,' said Annie, feeling relieved that she had taken a step towards Cherry. She was spending quite a bit of her time with Maria and Zoë, but never felt really easy with them somehow.

She always felt that hidden in whatever Maria said to her was some sort of competition.

As she was dropped off at the Vicarage, Annie was looking forward to her ballet lesson with Miss Rodelle.

The house, which stood in a quiet, tree-lined crescent, seemed enormous for one family. Cherry had told her it was Victorian. It was red brick and had very deep windows and fancy bits at the edges of the roof.

Cherry met her on the doorstep with a big grin and showed her in.

Annie gazed about her at the large, gracious hall and the wide, sweeping staircase.

'Oh, what a lovely house!' she said. 'It's even better than I guessed it would be.'

Cherry seemed pleased she liked it, even though she didn't share Annie's enthusiasm.

'Come up to my bedroom. I'm dying to show you all my things.'

The girls raced upstairs, giggling as they tripped over one another. Annie knew she wasn't going to have much time at Cherry's house before they had to leave, so she meant to make the most of it.

She tried to be her friendliest, funniest, liveliest self now she had Cherry on her own. But the funny thing was, after about ten minutes, when the girls got chatting about school, Annie forgot all about trying.

'Pip's crazy, isn't she!' Annie exclaimed. 'She's late for everything. And she always looks as though she's come through a hedge on the way to school!'

'I know,' chuckled Cherry. 'But she's great fun!'

'Have you been friends with her long?'

'Yes, right from the start of last year.'

'Have you been to her house much?' asked Annie, feeling a teeny bit jealous.

'No, not at all,' Cherry replied.

Annie looked surprised.

'It's strange, isn't it? She's been here tons of times, but I've never been invited to her home. I suppose it's because Minsterley's so far out. She has quite a bus journey you know. No wonder she's late for school so often.'

'Oh I see,' said Annie. 'So she lives right out in the country?'

'Yes,' said Cherry. 'I think there is a nearer school but she wanted to come to Bishop's.'

Cherry took Annie downstairs to get drinks and biscuits. The Vicar was busy in his study, but Annie met Cherry's mother. She was an older mother, like her own, and Annie felt instantly at home with the large-boned woman with fading red hair.

A little later, Mrs Stevens drove the girls to an industrial estate just outside the town, and dropped them off in the middle of it, outside what looked like a factory unit. The estate was dingy and neglected-looking. Oil-streaks and piles of litter cascaded down the tarmac.

'Is this it?' gulped Annie.

'Sure is,' said Cherry cheerfully. 'Look, here's the sign.' She pointed up to a scruffy hanging board which enumerated the various businesses off this road. 'That's us – E.6: THE RODELLE SCHOOL OF DANCE.'

Now Annie could hear strains of music coming from the unit, which looked rather like an aeroplane hangar. Her heart sinking into her boots, she followed Cherry inside.

There weren't many other pupils about. She already knew Pip, who was hanging around until her Modern class later. There were two other girls – Rosie and Sarah – who were in Pre-elementary ballet, but no boys.

Soon, Annie had forgotten the rather grim surroundings and was laughing and joking with the small group of students. A bedraggled line of small children, in pink leotards and skirts, came clattering out of the studio.

Pip stretched her leg up against the wall and pressed her nose against it. 'Have a good class,' she said.

'Don't you do ballet?' Annie asked her.

'Yes, but I'm in a lower grade. I like tap best.'

Annie followed Cherry into the large, draughty studio. Unlike Miss Vane, who had taken no notice of her at all, Miss Rodelle came over and chatted to Annie for a couple of minutes, while the others warmed up.

'Your mother tells me you gained a very high distinction for your Grade Five,' she said. 'You must feel very proud of yourself.'

'Aye, I mean, yes, I was very pleased,' said Annie,

feeling a little shy of the young, but assured, teacher. Miss Rodelle posed a great contrast to her surroundings. Her make-up was immaculate and her fair hair smoothed back into a perfect French plait. She wore her short flared black skirt and figure-hugging black top with great elegance.

'We'd be glad to have you here,' went on Miss Rodelle, smiling. 'We're a young school, as you must know already, but we're going to go far.'

As Annie looked into her determined green eyes, she felt this was not at all unlikely. She enjoyed the lesson which followed immensely. Miss Rodelle was an exacting teacher, but, to Annie's relief, didn't have Miss Vane's irritability of temper.

But somehow the spell was broken when the students spilled out once more into the changing rooms. Annie became uncomfortably conscious of the bare, peeling walls, and the lack of furniture or pegs.

How different it had been at the Wenlock school, where there was every facility and the walls were overflowing with news and photographs of exam and festival successes.

Even the studios were quite different. Here there were no mirrors or barres. The students had to use chair-backs for their barre work, but at least there was a good floor. At the Wenlock school, the studio had been well-equipped, with floor to ceiling mirrors and a double barre running along two walls.

Annie suddenly came to. Cherry had been asking

her something and was now evidently waiting for a response.

'Pardon,' she said.

'I said, what d'you think?' repeated Cherry, grinning.

Annie hesitated. And Cherry noticed the hesitation. *Oh dear*, thought Annie, *this doesn't get any easier*.

'To be honest,' she said, 'I just don't know which school to choose. They both seem really good.'

In bed that night, Annie chewed it all over in her mind. She dropped off to sleep eventually, without feeling any closer to a solution.

But when she woke up next morning, an idea had formed in her mind. An idea which, if it came off, could bridge the gulf between the Wenlock Theatre School and Miss Rodelle's School of Dance.

· 3 ·

Annie's Plan

Annie felt happy to be able to push to the back of her mind the decision about which dance school to choose. All her energies were now focused on her new plan. If it came off, it would be wonderful.

Once at school, she made a bee-line for Cherry and Pip, who were standing talking near the main entrance.

'Hey!' she called. 'I've had this great idea.'

'Come on, then,' laughed Cherry. 'Let's hear it.'

'Right,' said Annie feeling as if she were about to make a speech. She took a breath. 'Why don't we start a Dance Club, here, at Bishop's? We could meet in lunch-hours, perhaps even after school.

29

What d'you think?'

'It's a great idea, Annie,' Pip said, straight away. 'But won't it take a lot of organizing?' She frowned and ran her fingers through her bobbed hair. 'You know how scatty I am!'

'I'm a good organizer,' said Annie, without any attempt at humility. 'I just need you to back me up.'

'We'll certainly do that,' said Cherry. 'It would be great having a club in school. My only worry is Mr Reynolds.'

'Oh,' said Annie. Mr Reynolds was the headteacher of the school and she had been there long enough already to realize he was not the easiest of people to persuade. But then Annie immediately looked on the bright side.

'I'm sure we can get round him,' she said. 'It's good for the school, surely, to have lots of clubs and societies.'

Cherry and Pip looked at each other. 'But *dancing*!' said Cherry. 'It's not really Mr Reynold's cup of tea at all. Now, if it had been computers, it would have been quite another story.'

'Well I'm not giving up before we start!' cried Annie, rather impatiently. 'Are you with me, or not?'

'With you!' her friends replied together. They both giggled, slightly discomfited by Annie's outburst.

'Fine,' said Annie, the flush in her cheeks fading. 'Where do we go from here?'

Cherry considered. 'I think Mrs Race would be

the best person to ask, especially as we'll probably need the gym.'

'Right,' said Annie, consulting her timetable. 'Do we have PE today?'

'Yes. Last double lesson,' said Pip.

Cherry looked at her in surprise.

'I only remember because it was this time last week I was put in detention for forgetting my games kit.'

'Have you remembered it today?' Cherry asked.

'Yeh. No prob. I tied a knot in my tie.'

Pip showed them the thin end of her tie with the knot in it, then concealed it again behind the wider front part.

The bell went for first lesson, which was history. The girls took their bags along with them to the history room.

'So we'll ask Mrs Race in the games lesson,' said Annie, wanting to get things settled.

'OK,' said Cherry. 'I'm sure she'll be on our side. She loves dance – she does creative dance with us now and then.'

The girls' chatter had to stop when their history teacher, Mrs Mander, came in. She had a lot of pictures to show them of Tutankhamun and the Great Pyramids. They were studying Ancient Egypt.

Sam asked a lot of questions about the photographs. He seemed totally fascinated by them. Mrs Mander seemed really pleased he was so interested.

'Sam's usually so laid-back in history, he might as well be lying down,' whispered Cherry.

'Well, he seems pretty keen today,' said Annie.

'Yeh, I can't get over it,' said Cherry.

'Perhaps Ancient Egypt has cast a spell over him,' said Annie, posing her hands in Egyptian fashion and waggling her head from side to side.

Cherry giggled, but had to contain herself when Mrs Mander gave her a sharp look. They had to spend the rest of the lesson writing up notes in silence.

At the end of the class, they all spilled out into the corridor, moving to their next lesson. Annie found herself next to Sam.

'You seemed pretty interested in Ancient Egypt,' she commented.

'Nah,' said Sam. 'History's a load of rubbish. It's the here and now what interests me.'

'But you asked all those questions about the Pyramids and tombs?'

'That's 'cause I was interested in the *photographs*,' said Sam. 'They were fantastic, weren't they?'

'By the way,' said Annie, trying to sound casual, 'we're thinking of starting a Dance Club in school. If Mrs Race agrees, we'll try and have a meeting tomorrow lunch-time. Could you spread the word?'

'Sure,' said Sam. 'I'll let Maria and the others know about it. I like the idea of a dance club. More chance to practise!'

Annie felt relieved Sam was going to approach Maria. She hadn't had much to do with her since the visit to Miss Rodelle's dancing school. And in any case, Annie didn't want to be asked probing questions about whether she'd made up her mind, just at the moment.

Annie found an opportunity to speak to Mrs Race about the Dance Club when the young teacher came into the changing rooms just before the PE lesson.

'I think it's a wonderful idea,' said Mrs Race. 'Only I have so many commitments already with Gym Club and hockey and netball matches that I just don't think I could take anything extra on!'

'We realized that,' said Cherry tactfully, 'so we thought ...'

'We want to run it ourselves!' Annie burst in.

Mrs Race looked surprised. 'What sort of dance would it be then? You do ballet, don't you?'

'Aye,' said Annie, 'there'd be quite a lot of ballet, but we'd want to include Modern and tap and National.'

'Probably some singing and drama as well,' added Pip.

'Put on shows, musicals, that sort of thing,' said Cherry.

'And you three propose to run it?' said Mrs Race. She paused and considered, a wrinkle in her brow disturbing the smoothness of her tanned face. 'Well,' she said, 'I could make sure the gym's free for you a couple of times a week ...'

'Thanks, Mrs Race!' cried Annie, before she could finish.

'... but of course Mr Reynolds has the final say on such matters.'

The three friends looked so immediately downcast that the PE teacher laughed. 'I'll put in a good word for you, don't worry. For the moment, you'd better find out how many takers you have, to see if it's worth organizing.'

At lunch-time the following day, the friends called a meeting for anyone in Lower School who was interested. Annie presided as chairman and Cherry took notes.

They were pleased to see there was a good level of support for their plan. To Annie's relief, Sam had managed to persuade the other Wenlock dancers to come. Maria and Zoë were the first to arrive and sat right in front of Annie and Cherry, which Annie found a little disconcerting.

The twins, Kim and Susie Dorricott, followed along with four or five other Year 7 children, who didn't go to dancing classes, but who were interested in joining the club.

'That's twelve altogether,' said Cherry, with satisfaction, after jotting down everyone's name.

'It should help us in persuading Mr Reynolds,' whispered Pip.

Annie banged the table for silence, and then outlined the sort of activities the Dance Club would provide.

'Any questions?' she asked, after this intro-duction.

'Yes,' said Maria, immediately. 'Have you got Mr

Reynolds' permission yet?'

'Nay,' said Annie, 'but Mrs Race is behind us. I'm sure she'll get him to agree.'

'Another thing,' said Maria. 'Who exactly is going to be leading the sessions?'

'We'd share it between us, according to expertise. So if it was a Modern class, Cherry here would be in charge. If it was ballet, I would do it. If we were rehearsing a musical, say, Pip would coach the singing …'

As soon as she had spoken, Annie knew she had said the wrong thing. Maria not only saw herself as the leading ballet dancer among them, but also the star singer in the school.

'So it's all decided before we even start,' muttered Maria, her dark eyes glinting.

'Nay,' said Annie, 'we'll use the talent we have in the best way. Everyone'll get a chance to contribute in some way. That's the whole idea of a club!'

Maria fell silent, but Annie could tell she was only partly appeased. Next came a question about the club meeting times.

'We thought two lunch-times a week,' said Annie. 'And an after-school slot when we're rehearsing for a show.'

'Will there be any rules?' asked one of the twins. (Annie wasn't sure which one.)

'Just a few,' said Annie. 'Cherry has done a sheet for you on the word processor which mentions the rules. Just things like footwear, suitable clothing. Most of you have dance wear already anyway.'

35

'Shall we have a logo?' Sam suggested.

'Aye, that's a great idea, Sam. Perhaps you could design one for us?'

'Sure.'

'Could we have it printed on a T-shirt?' asked Pip. 'Then it could be our sort of uniform. It wouldn't matter then if we'd all got different coloured leotards.'

'Terrific,' said Annie. 'Are you getting all this down?' she asked Cherry.

'I think so,' said Cherry.

'Any other comments and questions?' Annie asked.

'Where would we be able to put on a show?' asked one of the twins.

'Well, school would be the obvious place,' said Annie, 'to start with at least.'

'If Mr Reynolds gives us permission,' Maria jabbed in.

'Of course,' said Annie smoothly, trying not to be ruffled. 'But then, as we get really into it, we could be more adventurous.'

'Do one in the scout hut!' muttered Zoë sarcastically, but loudly enough for Annie to hear. Maria and she burst into giggles.

'We might be invited to summer fêtes or carnivals or things like that!' Pip broke in. 'As our name grows.'

'Aye,' said Annie. 'That's just the sort of thing I was thinking of. Well, I think that's all for today. As soon as we get the go-ahead, we'll put a notice up

36

outside the gym, about which lunch-times we'll meet.'

The meeting broke up into small groups of gabbling girls and boys. Annie, Pip and Cherry were the last to leave the classroom.

'It went well, didn't it?' said Cherry.

'Aye, we had a good response,' said Annie. 'It was nice so many of the younger ones came, even though they don't go to dancing lessons.'

Pip frowned. 'It could make our job harder though,' she said.

'Dinna worry,' said Annie. 'It'll be fine, you'll see. It'll be quite different from lessons, where we're always preparing for exams and things. This will be for *fun*!'

'I'm all for that!' laughed Cherry.

'Another thing that worries me,' Pip went on.

Annie and Cherry groaned. 'What?'

'Maria and Zoë,' said Pip. 'They're going to be awkward, I can tell.'

'They'll stop trying to throw their weight around when we get down to the dancing,' said Annie breezily.

'I'm not so sure,' said Cherry. 'Maria has always been trouble. She's not going to change now.'

'Oh I don't know,' said Annie. 'When people are enjoying themselves, it's amazing how they fit in.'

'Well I shall be amazed if Maria and Zoë fit in,' said Pip. 'Still, it would be very difficult for us to bar them.'

'Anyway,' said Annie, 'I might decide to go to the

Wenlock school yet. Then Maria will be all over me.'

'Oh Annie!' cried Cherry. 'I thought you'd decided to come to Miss Rodelle's!'

'Sorry,' said Annie sheepishly. 'I shouldn't have mentioned it.' She sighed. 'To tell you the truth, I'm still finding it impossible to make up my mind.'

· 4 ·

Setbacks

It was another week before Mrs Race had an answer for them. The friends had pestered her every day, but she would only say that Mr Reynolds was still considering their request.

When the answer did come, it was not the definite yes they'd hoped for.

Mrs Race took Annie, Pip and Cherry on one side after their gym lesson.

'Mr Reynolds wants to see you personally, to find out more about your plans for the Dance Club,' she explained.

'Hasn't he made up his mind then?' asked Annie,

trying to keep her feeling of impatience out of her voice.

'No,' said Mrs Race, running her fingers through her short fair hair. 'I'm afraid he hasn't. I've been doing my best to persuade him, but he says he really needs to find out more from you.'

Mrs Race told them the time of their appointment with the head, and at 12.30 they were walking into his office.

He stood up and greeted them. Annie had never had a conversation with him before and felt a little nervous, especially as so much was at stake. She was very conscious they must make a good impression.

After Mr Reynolds had quizzed them for about ten minutes, he put his fingertips together on the desk in front of him, and looked at them steadily through black-framed spectacles. Annie still felt nervous. He had done little to put the girls at their ease. Annie thought he seemed a distant, even cold, man.

'I've heard all you have told me,' he said, after a long pause. 'And I shall give it my full consideration in due course. Is there anything else you would like to say?'

Annie opened her mouth to speak, but Cherry quickly trod on her foot. She had noticed the warning flush in her friend's cheeks. Annie closed her mouth quickly. Cherry was right. You had to be very careful what you said to Mr Reynolds.

'No thank you, Mr Reynolds,' Cherry was saying politely. Annie and Pip echoed her and they were all dismissed.

'Phew!' said Annie, crossing the hall. 'You saved me there, Cherry. Thanks!'

Cherry looked at her. 'What were you going to say? I could tell you were getting steamed up.'

'Oh, something like, "Haven't you had enough time, you old stick insect? It doesn't take *this* long to make up your mind surely?" '

The friends burst into giggles.

'I'd like to have seen his face!' cried Pip, between convulsive bursts of laughter.

'Anyway,' said Cherry, when they'd all calmed down. 'You're a good one to complain, Annie. I can think of something it's taken you a long time to make your mind up about!'

'Point taken,' said Annie, without looking at all abashed. 'Actually, I *have* made up my mind now.'

'You have!' cried Cherry. 'Oh tell us, quick!'

'Tell you tomorrow,' said Annie, 'in case I change my mind.' She gave them a wicked grin.

'Stop teasing!' exclaimed Pip. 'And tell us.'

'I've decided to come to …' Annie paused and gave them another grin.

'Oh Annie!' cried Cherry, in an agony of waiting.

'Miss Rodelle's!' Annie announced triumphantly.

'Great! Fantastic!' her friends chorused giving her bear-hugs.

By now they had moved outside, on to the yard. Other pupils stared as they linked hands and charged round in a circle, shouting and whooping like mad things.

Annie was not much less excited when she arrived at Miss Rodelle's a couple of nights later for her first ballet lesson. Unlike her first visit, she didn't really notice the depressing surroundings or the tatty changing rooms. She was far too busy chatting to Cherry about dancing matters.

When it was time to go in for their lesson, Annie had to see Miss Rodelle to order two new leotards. The school took examinations with a different board from her last school. In the Pre-elementary class here she would need black, not navy blue. She also needed a new pair of flat ballet shoes.

'What about pointe shoes?' asked Miss Rodelle. 'Have you any yet?'

'No,' Annie admitted. 'My last teacher wouldn't put us on pointe till we'd been in the class a full twelve months.'

'Very wise of her,' Miss Rodelle answered. 'I'll have a good look at you today, to see if you're ready for pointe work.'

When she smiled warmly, Annie felt glad she had decided to come to her classes.

During the lesson, conscious of the young teacher's eyes upon her, she felt a little flustered. She was rather out of practice. Her leg muscles particularly had stiffened and weakened. She found steps she normally found easy difficult.

In particular, when they were doing échappés and relevés, her demi-pointes felt a little unsteady. Normally they felt rock solid. She and Cherry had a chance to watch the more experienced girls in the class doing the same exercise on full pointe.

Annie had a pang of longing. Ever since she was a very small girl she had longed to dance on her toes. She had been taken to the theatre when she was only five to see *The Nutcracker*, and had thought that to dance like the Sugar Plum Fairy was to reach some kind of heaven.

She hoped against hope that Miss Rodelle would agree to order some blocked toe shoes for her at the end of the lesson. But instead, Miss Rodelle said, 'I don't think your feet and legs are quite strong enough yet for pointe work. It is so important to get these things right.'

Annie tried hard not to show how disappointed she felt, but Miss Rodelle must have noticed.

'Work hard, and we'll build up your strength. You've got perfect legs and feet for ballet,' she said kindly. 'And you wouldn't thank me if I let you damage them for the rest of your life.'

An image of Miss Vane's awful bunions suddenly flashed into Annie's mind. 'No, Miss Rodelle,' she said, with sincerity.

She vowed to herself that she would do an hour's practice at home every day from now on. Pointe shoes would be a marvellous reward.

Annie enjoyed all her other dance classes at her new school. For National Dance, Miss Rodelle decided to fit her in with a group of girls (which included Pip) who were to take their silver medal in only a month's time.

'I can see you have a flair for National Dance,'

said Miss Rodelle. 'I see no reason why you shouldn't go in for your Silver at the beginning of October. You're almost up to standard already. And then you can start working towards your Gold.'

Delighted at this unexpected opportunity, Annie made a mental note to start practising her National dances for at least half an hour a day. Life was going to get very busy!

Annie had Cherry's company in all three of her other subjects – they were both Pre-elementary standard in ballet and Modern, and Grade 5 in tap. Pip joined them for tap, but she was only in Grade 4 for Modern. She had not been blessed with a particularly flexible or graceful body, whereas she excelled at the fast footwork of tap lessons.

'What did you think of your first week with us?' asked Cherry on Friday evening. The three girls were walking back to Cherry's after their tap lesson.

'It's been fine,' said Annie. 'Really good. I just wish we could get on with the Dance Club now.'

Annie had her wish, for first thing on Monday morning, Mrs Clanger told them that Mr Reynolds wanted to speak to the three of them straight after assembly.

When they went to see him, he peered at them over his heavy glasses. 'I want to make it quite clear,' he said, 'that any bad behaviour whatsoever will lead to an immediate ban on the club meetings. In other words, you three are directly responsible for keeping the younger ones in order.'

'Yes, Mr Reynolds,' Annie answered. 'I think we'll

44

keep them so busy they won't have time to think about playing up.'

Mr Reynolds gave her a look. 'That remains to be seen, doesn't it, young lady? Meanwhile Mrs Race will tell you which lunch-times the gym is free.'

The girls thanked the headteacher and moved towards the door.

'One more thing,' he said, 'I'm giving you a privilege which would usually only be offered to our older students. Use it wisely. You are very much on probation.'

Despite Mr Reynolds' warning, the friends were delighted that at last they could go ahead with their plans. The very next lunch-time, they had their first Dance Club session. It was attended by all the people who had gone to the initial meeting, plus a few extra friends who had been persuaded to come along.

Annie's butterflies soon settled once she got going with the warm-up exercises she was showing everyone. The girls had brought a tape recorder with them and played a pop song from the Top Ten which everyone was humming at the moment. The regular beat was ideal for Annie's warm-ups.

After ten minutes, they paused for a rest. 'We thought we'd do a Modern session today,' she explained to everyone, 'and then ballet on Thursday. Any questions?'

'Yes,' said Maria immediately. 'Would you like me to take the ballet class? I'm probably the best qualified to do it.'

'Er, fine,' said Annie, reluctantly. 'But I better make it clear that Mr Reynolds has put us three in charge of the club. We have the final say on all club matters.'

Maria's mouth set hard.

'Be careful,' Cherry whispered in Annie's ear. 'We don't want them all to think we're being too bossy.'

But Annie found it difficult not to react to Maria's challenges. It was probably just as well that Cherry took over the lead just then.

Cherry took them through their paces to some very fast modern jazz. The untrained children got in a serious muddle a lot of the time. By the end they were bent double, gasping for breath. Even the girls and boys who knew what they were doing were exhausted.

'I think you went a bit OTT,' panted Pip.

'What?' asked Cherry, who looked aglow with health.

'You know. Over The Top. We're all shattered. And the poor '*ducklings*'!' (This was the friends' name for the untrained recruits.) 'Well, just look at them!'

The sight of them was certainly more eloquent than words could be. They were slumped against walls or lying flat out on the floor.

'Oops!' said Cherry. 'I was enjoying myself so much I didn't realize!'

'Never mind,' said Annie. 'We'll all have things to learn. You made it a very, um, *exciting* session.'

Maria approached the friends with Zoë.

'Oh-oh, here comes trouble,' said Pip.

'Sh,' said Annie. 'Did you enjoy that?' she asked the two girls as they came up.

'Yes and no,' said Maria.

'More no than yes,' added Zoë, who looked very red in the face and sweaty.

'Well, we must expect teething problems,' said Annie brightly.

'I wanted to ask you something,' said Maria.

'Fire away,' said Annie.

'It's been over a fortnight since you visited our dance school. I just wondered if you'd fixed anything up with Miss Vane yet.'

'Nay,' replied Annie, colouring a little. 'I decided against Wenlock.'

'Against Wenlock?' cried Zoë, as if this was unthinkable.

'That's right,' said Annie. 'It was really hard to decide between the two, but anyway, I've started at Miss Rodelle's now.'

'I see,' said Maria coldly. 'In that case there's nothing more to be said.'

'I hope we can still be friends,' said Annie. 'And of course we'll see lots of each other at Dance Club.'

'Come on, Zoë,' said Maria, turning her back on Annie.

At the next meeting, two days later, the three friends stood in the gym waiting for Maria to turn up. Everyone was getting impatient to start the ballet class. To the friends' surprise, all the

47

'ducklings' had come back. Most arrived in leotards of one shade or another, and a good half had begged or borrowed ballet shoes, many with plasters covering holes in the toes.

'She's ten minutes late,' hissed Cherry.

'Yes, even I was only a couple of minutes late today,' said Pip. 'And I'm not supposed to be leading.'

'I'll have to start it,' said Annie. 'She can take over when she decides to turn up. It'll probably cause an argument, but still.'

Annie switched on a tape of Chopin waltzes and directed people to various pieces of gym apparatus they could use as barres. She led them through pliés and tendues, trying to remember to explain everything clearly. She found she was good at spotting errors in posture and placing, which was very useful with the 'ducklings'.

She became so immersed in what she was doing that she was shocked when Cherry told her it was time to finish.

'What happened to Maria, I wonder?' said Annie, as she was taking off her ballet shoes.

'It's pretty obvious isn't it?' said Cherry. 'She's in a huff because you haven't joined the Wenlock Theatre School.'

'I didn't think she'd leave the club, though,' said Annie, frowning. 'Oh dear, why do things have to be so difficult?'

One of the 'ducklings' came up to her. 'Thanks Annie,' she said. 'That was great. I'm definitely going to stay in the club.'

'One satisfied customer at least,' said Pip.

When Annie got home that night, she encountered difficulties of a different sort. Because the problem of Maria was on her mind, she started talking to her mother about it, while her father was in the room. Normally she didn't discuss anything to do with her dancing life in front of him.

When he had picked up the fact that Annie had founded the Dance Club, he wanted to know all the details, especially regarding the time she would have to give to it.

'I'm nay happy,' he said at last. 'Your schoolwork comes first. I thought that was clear.'

'It is, Dad. It is,' said Annie, hoping the discussion would end there.

'Aren't there any other clubs you could join, run by the staff. Chess, computers, that sort of thing?'

'Aye, there are,' Annie answered. 'But you ken how keen I am on dancing and …'

'A passing phase, that's all,' Mr Macdonald cut in. 'You'll go through dozens of hobbies afore you're done.'

Annie thought it best not to point out that dancing had been her only hobby since before she started school.

'At least lunch-times shouldn't interfere with homework,' he said. 'But if I get a hint of anything slipping in that department, we may have to think again.'

In bed, Annie felt beset by worries. There was *You are responsible for their behaviour*, from Mr Reynolds. There was the unfortunate way Maria had taken Annie's decision to go to Miss Rodelle's. And now there was her father looking over her shoulder.

She would have to be very careful about her homework, especially if the club started having after-school practices.

· 5 ·

Persuasion

Annie decided to confront Maria. The opportunity came next morning in form-time, as Mrs Clanger was very late coming in to take their register.

'Where were you?' Annie asked. 'You were supposed to be leading the ballet class!'

Maria sniffed. 'I don't see why you expect any loyalty from me. Not *now*!'

'Oh don't be silly, Maria!' Annie exclaimed. 'It doesn't matter which dance school we belong to, or if we got to one at all for that matter! This is supposed to be a club for anyone with an interest, based here at Bishop's!'

'You're welcome to it,' said Maria, turning away.

'I choose not to come to the club any more.'

Annie sat down next to Cherry and sighed. 'I'm not going to get round *her* too easily, am I?'

'Don't know why you bothered,' said Cherry. 'You don't know Maria as well as I do.'

'But it's ridiculous!' cried Annie. 'Just because I didn't go to Wenlock.'

'It's what's she like,' said Cherry. 'We did warn you. I mean, she stopped speaking to us when we left.'

'We could do with her and Zoë in the club,' said Annie. 'They're both strong dancers.'

'I don't know,' said Cherry. 'I think we may be better off without them.'

Annie could not fully agree with Cherry, as she still held fast to her belief in the Dance Club as a uniting force. However, there was little she could do at the moment to try to change Maria's mind.

She had plenty of other things to think about, anyway. There was her National exam looming up for a start. And homework from school was starting to pile up.

By the time the next club meeting came round, Annie was looking forward to it as a time for relaxation and fun. Pip and Cherry were as enthusiastic as ever, and she began to regain some of her initial excitement as members started arriving at the gym.

Fifteen minutes later, her outlook had changed entirely. Not only were Maria and Zoë missing, but Sam, Kim, Susie and a couple of their friends also.

A very depleted Dance Club limped through the tap session Pip had prepared for them.

'Maria's been at work,' said Pip, at the end.

'Definitely,' said Cherry.

'I don't see why they've changed their minds,' said Annie, fretfully. 'I mean, Sam and the twins were so keen to help, and everything.'

'Don't worry about it, Annie,' said Cherry, putting her arm around her friend's shoulders. 'It's not your fault.'

'I know that,' said Annie, 'but I did so want everyone to make friends and work together.'

'Things don't always work out as you'd like them to,' said Cherry. 'We can still run the club, small though it is, and hope to build it up during the year.'

Annie sighed. She felt unable to let the matter rest there, but wasn't sure what she could do about it. One thing was clear in her mind, though. She was at least going to try. The rest of the day was spent racking her brains.

'Are you busy tomorrow after dancing?' she asked her friends at home-time.

'No, I don't think so,' answered Cherry.

'Why?' asked Pip.

'I wondered if you'd like to come round to my place. There's something I want to talk to you about.'

'Yes, love to,' said Cherry, quickly echoed by Pip.

When Annie led her two new friends down the

short drive to her house the next evening, she was apologetic.

'It's just a box,' she said. 'A small one at that. Nothing grand or graceful, like your vicarage, Cherry.'

'Doesn't worry me,' said Cherry. 'Our house is like a barn. Now the weather's turning cooler it's awful. Dad has such trouble with the boiler, he refuses to light it till well into October. So we freeze till then.' She shivered at the thought.

The friends walked round the side of the house, which was smothered with climbing roses and reddening Virginia creeper.

'Oh this is pretty!' cried Pip. 'More like a country garden.'

'Mum was determined to keep a cottage flavour, even though we're on an estate in town.'

'She must be a good gardener,' said Pip, admiring the late blooms.

'Have you got a nice garden?' asked Annie. 'I suppose it's all countrified, living where you do?'

'Um, yes, I like it,' said Pip.

'Is it big?' asked Cherry curiously. She had never managed to get much information out of Pip on the subject.

'Oh, aren't these roses *gorgeous*!' exclaimed Pip, ignoring her.

Annie let them in through the back door which led into the kitchen. Mrs Macdonald was baking bread, and had to wipe her hands when Annie introduced her friends.

'That's a gorgeous smell!' cried Pip.

'And it's so *warm* in here!' said Cherry.

Annie laughed. 'Don't forget Mum's got the oven on.' She showed them up to her room.

'Wow, this is tidy!' said Pip. 'You should see mine. You can't see the floor for clothes and junk!'

Indeed Annie's room was tidy and well-organized. There were two baskets on her dressing table, which held all her bits and bobs. Apart from books, a few ornaments and cuddly toys, everything else was out of sight, with the exception of a pen-tidy and a single exercise book on her desk. Cherry picked the book up and read the title Annie had written on its cover – *The Dance Club*.

'It's my ideas book,' Annie explained.

'I like your posters,' said Pip. Annie had two enormous pictures of Bolshoi Ballet stars on her wall.

'Is that what you want to be?' she asked Annie.

'Of course,' she said. 'It's a dream, isn't it? But we all know the odds against it happening.'

'What about you?' asked Pip, turning now to Cherry. 'Do you want to be a dancer too?'

'I don't know,' Cherry answered. 'I really don't. Some days I think I'd like it, others I know I'd hate it.'

'Well, what would you do if you didn't go into dancing?' asked Annie.

'Something to do with sport probably,' answered Cherry. 'Jumping for Britain in the Olympics, for instance!' She giggled.

'Come on then, Pip,' said Annie. 'Tell us your ambitions.'

'I'm more like Cherry,' answered Pip. 'I'm not sure. I know I wouldn't make it as a dancer, but singing, well, maybe there's just a chance of getting somewhere with that!'

'I haven't heard you sing yet,' said Annie.

'She's got a fantastic voice!' Cherry broke in.

'Sing something now for us,' asked Annie.

'Oh no,' said Pip shyly. 'Your mum and dad might hear. And anyway, what was it you wanted to talk to us about?'

Annie laughed. 'You don't find out till you give us a song.'

So Pip sang them 'A Whole New World' from *Aladdin*, in a tuneful soprano, which was sweet, but none the less powerful. Her friends burst into applause.

'That was lovely!' cried Annie. 'With a voice like that, the sky's the limit.'

As Pip smiled at them gratefully, Annie thought to herself, *here's a budding talent I need to encourage.*

'Do you sing solos in school concerts and things?' she asked.

'No,' said Pip. 'Not at school.'

'Why ever not?'

'I'll tell you why not,' said Cherry. 'Because Miss Maria Farran always gets the spotlight!'

'Has she got a really good voice?' asked Annie.

'Yes, but nowhere near as good as Pip's. She's just more up-front about it. And she can twist the music

56

teachers round her little finger!'

'I wanted to talk to you about Maria,' said Annie.

The others groaned. 'We thought it was going to be something exciting,' Cherry complained.

'Have either of you had a chance to speak to Sam or the twins yet?' Annie asked.

'Not the twins,' said Pip, 'but I had a few words with Sam. He said he was following Maria – Wenlock dancers sticking together, that sort of thing.'

'Sounds like she can twist Sam round her little finger too,' said Annie. 'But, let me tell you the plan I've thought up.'

She picked up the notebook from the bed, where Cherry had dropped it.

'What do you think about working towards a show straight away?'

'We were going to get the club established first,' Cherry reminded her.

'I know,' said Annie. 'This is a bit of a gamble, really. I'm banking on it being a pull to get the Wenlock kids back in the club.'

'It might work,' said Pip. 'But Maria's awfully stubborn.'

'But how about if we offer Maria a star part. Appeal to her vanity?'

'I think we should have a go,' said Cherry. 'It's a brilliant idea!'

'Have you worked out what we could do in a show?' asked Pip.

Annie flicked through her notes. 'I've been thinking about a shortish ballet, for everyone to join in and I came up with the idea of a magic toyshop. You know, all the different toys coming to life at night. Then we could do some nice simple dances for the "ducklings".'

'Yeah, they could be clockwork mice and scuttle around the stage!' said Cherry with a chuckle.

'That sort of thing,' said Annie. 'And I'm hoping we'll get Sam back. I want him to be the magician that starts off all the magic. A bit like Drosselmeyer in *The Nutcracker*.'

'That would appeal to him, I'm sure,' said Pip. 'Yes, it's a really good idea.'

'What about the other parts?' asked Cherry.

'Well, I fancied being a Scottish doll, then I could do one of my National solos. And I thought we could entice Maria with a Spanish solo – she's supposed to be very good at Spanish dancing, isn't she?'

'Yes,' said Cherry. 'I'm sure it'll work. I can't imagine Maria ever turning down the chance to do a solo.'

'And the twins would make a perfect pair of rag dolls,' went on Annie.

'What have you got lined up for me?' asked Cherry with a giggle.

Annie hesitated. 'How would you like to be the Christmas tree angel?' she asked, slightly nervously. Seeing Cherry's face, she hurried on. 'I know it's not quite you, but I need someone good at ballet, and you look the part, with your lovely hair.'

'It won't do my sporting image a lot of good,' said Cherry, giggling, 'but so what? I'll do it!'

'Thanks,' said Annie, with relief. 'Now for Pip. How would you like to be the teddy-bear?'

'Great,' said Pip. 'I've always wanted to be Sooty!' Annie laughed.

'So what about Zoë and the 'ducklings'?' Cherry asked.

'Oh there are lots of possibilities: sailors dolls for the younger boys – we can teach them a simple hornpipe; a couple of jack-in-the-boxes to leap up now and then.'

'Perhaps Maria and Zoë could be a pantomime horse?' suggested Pip innocently.

The others laughed at the image that conjured up.

'Apart from the Magic Toyshop,' Annie went on, when they'd recovered themselves, 'I'd like some of us to do a short tap dance, with your help, Pip, and also a number from a musical. Any ideas?'

'Oh, I know, I know!' cried Pip excitedly. *West Side Story*. It's fantastic!'

'Which bit d'you fancy?'

'Well, as we're mainly girls, 'I Feel Pretty', is probably the best bet,' Pip replied. 'But I'd love to do the duet, 'Somewhere',' she added wistfully.

'I guess you and Maria could manage it,' said Annie. 'Let's do it as well.'

'No,' said Pip. 'It would ruin it having two girls.'

'Don't you remember?' Cherry broke in. 'Sam has a really good voice. I bet he could sing Tony's part to your "Maria"!'

Pip's face lit up. 'Oh, I'd give anything to sing it!'

59

'Then you shall!' Annie said.

Pip frowned suddenly. 'But we don't know yet for sure if we can even *have* a show at school!' she said.

'I'll ask Mrs Race tomorrow,' said Annie. 'Cross your fingers and toes!'

Annie sought out the PE teacher first thing next morning to make her request. Mrs Race was all in favour of their idea. She knew that the head of music, Mr Farr was arranging a mid-term concert for the choir and concert band.

'I gather he hasn't enough items yet for a full programme,' said Mrs Race. 'He was talking to me about it only the other day, so you might be in luck. I'll have a word with him and Mr Reynolds, of course.'

This sounded distinctly hopeful, and the friends spent the rest of the day with a feeling of high expectation. For once, they were not disappointed. Mr Farr and the headteacher had both agreed in principle, though both wished to watch a rehearsal nearer the time.

'I suppose they're frightened we'll be a load of rubbish,' said Annie.

'Well, you can see their point,' said Cherry. 'We *are* a bit of an unknown factor.'

'We'll *have* to make a success of this one,' said Annie. 'It's a great opportunity. We mustn't miss it.'

'Now all we need is some bodies to put in the show!' Pip reminded them.

Annie worked on Maria first. She knew it was useless to try to get Sam and the twins to come back

60

on their own. She 'buttered her up' as much as she could bear, without feeling physically sick. Then she went on to describe the wonderful show they were going to present in the mid-term concert for pupils and parents.

Annie could see that Maria was trying hard not to look interested. *Now for the final bait*, she thought to herself.

'And we're planning a lovely part for you in the Magic Toyshop, Maria.'

'Oh, what is it?' Maria asked, despite herself. Zoë, too, looked interested.

'Well, of course, it's secret among club members for now,' said Annie cleverly. 'But if you turn up at the next meeting, I'll tell you all about it then! And your part, too, Zoë.'

Maria's face turned sulky.

'We're starting rehearsals straight away,' Annie pressed on, while she had the advantage. 'So it's really important everyone's there on Tuesday, when the parts get allocated.'

Maria swallowed hard. 'I'll have to think about it,' she said.

'Yeah,' said Zoë. 'We'll think about it.'

'Fine,' said Annie. 'It's going to be a great show.'

The friends didn't catch up with the other Wenlock dancers until the long break at lunchtime. Cherry and Pip spotted the twins and went off to try their luck with them, while Annie hovered on the edge of the yard, waiting for Sam to stop kicking a football around with his friends. At last he came off for a breather, and Annie was able to intercept him. She told him all about the Dance Club's plans for a show.

'We'd really like you to take the part of the magician,' said Annie. 'Sort of Drosselmeyer, you know. Lots of swirling your cape around and looking mysterious.'

'Sounds great,' said Sam, 'but I don't know if ...'

'I'm pretty sure Maria and Zoë are coming back,' Annie interjected.

'Oh,' said Sam, looking surprised. 'Well, in that case ...'

'And how about singing "Somewhere", the duet from *West Side Story*, with Pip?'

'Yeah, now you're talking,' said Sam with a huge grin. 'I'd love to do that.'

· 6 ·

Trouble at Rehearsals

Just as Annie had hoped, all the Wenlock dancers turned up to the Tuesday club meeting. Sam and the twins looked a little sheepish, but Annie and her friends gave them all a welcoming smile.

Sam had come in with a fair-haired boy, who Annie didn't recognize. He was taller than Sam by a head.

'Who's that?' she whispered to Cherry.

'Robbie Timpson,' Cherry whispered back. 'He's a mate of Sam's. Didn't know he was into dancing, though.'

Sam came across just then to ask them if it was all right to bring his friend.

'Of course,' said Annie. 'It's great to have another boy in the club.'

'He's never been to a dancing lesson in his life,' said Sam, 'but he's always wanted to have a go.'

'Well, now's his big chance,' laughed Pip.

'Right, we'd better start the meeting,' said Annie, seeing everyone had arrived.

First she explained her ideas for the Magic Toyshop and gave out the parts. There was a ripple of excitement when she'd finished talking.

Even Maria seemed satisfied, as Annie expected her to be, with her part as the Spanish doll. Her solo was to be one of the longest in the ballet, matched only by Annie's own Highland Fling and Cherry's dance as the Christmas angel.

But Maria, being Maria, had to have a moan about *something*. 'How is it,' she began, 'that some people already knew about their parts, even though they were supposed to be a big secret till today?'

'Must have slipped out somehow,' said Annie airily. 'But don't worry, Maria, we all know now, don't we?'

'Are we doing anything else besides the ballet?' asked Sam's friend, Robbie.

'Yes,' Annie replied. 'Those of us who can will do a short tap item, and we're also hoping to put on an excerpt from *West Side Story*.'

'Can we do the Jets and Sharks bit?' asked one of the twins. 'It's fantastic music!'

'We haven't decided yet,' Annie answered. 'But

that's a good suggestion, er—?' (She looked at Cherry helplessly, still unable to tell the sisters apart.) 'We certainly want a number for everyone to join in, and we're also thinking of doing the duet, 'Somewhere', with Pip singing Maria and Sam as Tony.'

'You can't be serious!' Maria called out suddenly. 'Pip looks completely wrong for the role. *Maria* has to have Latin looks, like me. Plus the fact that Pip has no experience of singing big parts, has she?'

'No,' Zoë agreed. 'She's never even sung a solo with the choir.'

Annie bit back the retort that came to her lips and looked across at Pip. Her friend had gone very pale and looked as if she didn't know what to do with her hands.

'Cherry and I are sure Pip will do fine in the part,' said Annie firmly, and quickly steered the meeting into some work for the group scenes in the Magic Toyshop. Clowns had been added to the list of toys, so that their comic antics gave an extra dimension of movement.

As Annie directed the jack-in-the-boxes to pop up, and the clockwork mice to run about the stage, she wondered if it would ever look organized. At the moment it was sheer chaos, especially when the clowns started their tumbling. She had decided on a very energetic finale, using Offenbach's cancan music, but only had time to show them the first few bars of it.

'Gosh, that rehearsal whizzed by,' said Cherry, as

they moved into the changing room.

'It did, didn't it?' said Annie. 'Makes you realize how long it's all going to take. We'll have to see Mrs Race and start booking the gym for extra sessions. Or the drama room, for coaching solos and duets.'

'It's exciting, isn't it?' said Pip. 'I think everything's going really well.'

Maria walked up to the group of friends, Zoë tailing as always. She drew Annie on one side.

'I think we need to finish talking about the *West Side Story* duet.'

'I thought we *had* finished,' said Annie.

'No, I don't think so,' said Maria. 'That part was *made* for me! If I don't have it, I'm backing out of the whole thing.'

'Maria! You wouldn't!' cried Annie, shocked.

'And don't be surprised if others follow. It happened once before, don't forget.'

'I couldn't take the part away from Pip now,' said Annie. 'It wouldn't be fair. She's set her heart on it.'

'So have I,' said Maria, looking very determined. 'What's it to be – a show with me singing *Maria* or no show? The choice is yours.'

Annie for once was lost for words.

Maria sniffed. 'Tell me when you've made up your mind. Might see you on Thursday.' She lugged her bag over her shoulder and flounced out of the changing rooms.

'Well, of all the cheek!' said Annie. 'Did you hear that?'

Cherry and Pip had overheard everything. 'I

suspected this might happen,' said Pip. 'But I just pretended to myself it wouldn't.'

'I suppose we were daft thinking everything was going to be rosy, with Maria around,' said Cherry.

'Look,' said Pip, 'if it's going to prevent problems, I'll give up the part willingly.'

'Oh Pip, you know how excited you were about it!' Annie exclaimed.

Pip shrugged, but Annie guessed how much it was costing her to make the offer.

'We can't let you do this!' said Annie.

'No we can't,' Cherry agreed. 'Quite apart from it not being fair on you, if we give in to Maria now, she'll try the same thing every time we have a show.'

'If only the others weren't so influenced by her!' cried Annie. 'I suppose she'll carry out her threat to persuade them to leave again?'

'I'm sure she will,' said Cherry. 'And she'll more than likely succeed.'

Immediately after lunch was a single lesson of history. Mrs Mander was absent, so a supply teacher sat in while the class got on with some set written work. Annie's mind refused to stay on Tutankhamun. She just kept going over and over the new dilemma Maria had presented her with. By the time the lesson was over, her head was spinning.

Fortunately they had games next. Fresh air coupled with tearing around the netball court made her feel a lot better. But at the end of the session, when they were walking back to the changing rooms, Mrs Race caught up with the friends.

'I've been meaning to ask how your Dance Club's going?' she said in a friendly way.

'Oh – er – fine,' said Annie.

'No teething problems?'

'Well, just a few,' Annie admitted cautiously.

'But nothing you can't handle?'

'No, nothing,' Annie replied. Their last conversation with Mr Reynolds came flooding back. If he found out that there were already quarrels and problems, Annie knew that the club would be short-lived indeed.

'I thought I might pop in next week,' went on Mrs Race. 'Mr Reynolds asked me to keep an eye on things, you know. You don't mind, do you?'

'Er no, Mrs Race,' said Cherry. Annie felt her heart sinking into her boots. Whatever was she going to do? She hated to disappoint one of her best friends. She hated giving into Maria's blackmail. But if she didn't was there ever going to be a club, let alone a show?

She made her decision right then and there, and told her friends about it in the changing rooms.

'I think it's the wrong thing to do,' said Cherry, 'but of course I'll back you if you think it's the only way.'

Annie had banked on this. Cherry rarely opposed her for long.

Pip was looking miserable.

'I'm really sorry, Pip,' said Annie. 'I promise I'll

make it up to you in our next show.'

'Don't worry, Annie. I know there'll be other opportunities. The main thing at the moment is to get the club launched and the show on the road!'

Annie hugged her. 'You're a great friend!' she said.

There was a triumphant glint in Maria's eyes when Annie and Cherry told her she could have the part. The friends rushed off as quickly as they could, not able to bear listening to her gloating.

'I hope you know what you're doing,' said Cherry.

'Once the club's up and running, she'll start to lose her influence over Sam and the twins, you'll see,' said Annie.

'And Zoë?'

Annie giggled. 'That's asking too much. They're like Tweedledum and Tweedledee.'

The next club meeting went amazingly smoothly. Maria kept her mouth shut, and they got down to rehearsal almost immediately. Annie saw the beginnings of improvement in the scenes she was rehearsing from the Magic Toyshop. She began to feel more confident about Mrs Race popping in for a look the following week.

Sam and Robbie came to see her at the end of the meeting.

'What do you think of this for a logo?' Sam asked, holding up his design for her, Cherry and Pip to study. It was simple, but striking – a ballet shoe on pointe, resting against a tap shoe.

'Oh it's fantastic, Sam!' said Annie.

'Yeah, it really gets across there's different types of dancing going on,' said Robbie.

It was the first time Annie had ever really spoken to Sam's friend, and the first time she had noticed what a nice smile he had. Not a huge, face-splitting grin like Sam's, more a quick, shy smile.

Cherry and Pip both loved the design, as did the twins, who had by now joined the group.

'We know someone who prints T-shirts, don't we, Susie?' said Kim.

'Yes,' her sister agreed. 'If we wanted to order some for the club, we could go and see him.'

'Great,' said Annie.

At the next meeting, the twins reported that their neighbour had agreed to print a dozen T-shirts for the club at a knock-down price.

Annie called Sam over and told him to pass on the design to Kim and Susie.

'Then all we need to do is decide on a colour,' she said.

'Fine,' said Sam. Annie couldn't help noticing his eyes were rather red-rimmed.

'What's the matter with Sam?' she asked Pip when he'd moved away.

'I don't know,' said Pip. 'But he's been very quiet the last couple of days.'

Annie got everyone to sit down, so they could have suggestions for the T-shirt colour.

'First of all,' said Cherry. 'Is everyone sure they

want one? Luckily, they're not going to cost a lot.'

There was a cannon of yeses.

'OK,' said Annie. 'So what colour?'

Every colour of the rainbow was suggested, so the laborious process of voting was begun. In the end Robbie's proposal of black was just outvoted by Cherry's of purple. Maria looked thunder-faced that her own suggestion – pink – had been voted for only by herself and Zoë.

'Thank heavens pink didn't win!' Cherry whispered. 'It would have looked awful with my red hair.'

'It'll be great having matching T-shirts,' said Annie. 'They'll do for our tap number in the show, too.'

At that moment, quite unexpectedly, Wayne and Darren, the older boys who had picked on Annie on her first morning at Bishop's, burst into the gym.

'What d'you think you two are doing here?' Annie asked. She looked round for support. Her friends had gathered round, with the exception of Sam, who seemed to have disappeared into thin air.

'It's a free country, innit?' said Wayne.

He and Darren swaggered around the gym, kicking out at apparatus mindlessly.

'I think we'll just get on with the rehearsal,' said Annie. 'Perhaps they'll get bored. Put the music on, Pip.'

As the music for their Magic Toyshop finale began, the two older boys linked arms and did a ridiculous version of the cancan with loud guffaws and shouts. The other children had to give their flailing arms and legs a very wide berth.

Annie stopped the music. 'Look, this is stupid. You're disturbing our rehearsal. You have no right to be here. Now please go!'

'Pleath go,' Darren mimicked, with a lisp.

'Who's going to make us?' said Wayne.

Annie's heart was beginning to thump. What should she do? She certainly didn't want to abandon the rehearsal. She tried once more to get started on one of the dances, but the boys made themselves more and more obnoxious. They plonked themselves by the tape recorder, shouldering Pip off her perch, and started switching it on and off.

'Where's Nooryef?' Wayne shouted.

'Yeah, we want Nooryef!' yelled Darren, smacking the palm of his hand on the table.

'Nooryef?' asked Annie, who was just longing for them to go.

'They mean Sam,' hissed Robbie from behind her. 'They're always after him.'

'I think I saw him go into the boys' changing rooms,' said one of the 'ducklings' innocently.

The boys jumped up immediately, and made for the door. Robbie intercepted them.

'No!' he shouted. 'Leave him alone. He hasn't done you any harm.'

Wayne laughed in his face and pushed him to one side.

'Out of my way, shrimp!' he cried.

'Stop that!' Annie yelled.

Robbie recovered his balance and launched himself on to Wayne's back. Everything happened really quickly after that. Hearing Robbie's yells, Sam came out of hiding to help his friend.

Wayne and Darren set about the two younger boys and it soon became clear they were overpowering them. Unable to stop the brawl, Annie and her friends, joined by some of the 'ducklings', pitched in to try to stop Sam and Robbie getting hurt.

The battle was at its fiercest when the main door to the gym opened. Annie just had the chance to see the look of horror on Mrs Race's face, before the scrum she was in collapsed. She banged her head on the wall and everything went black.

· 7 ·

A Burglary

When Annie came round, the first thing she was aware of was that she was in an ambulance. The face of the paramedic who was sitting beside her split into two. The inside of the ambulance appeared to spin slowly round to the right. She closed her eyes, feeling giddy and sick.

'You'll be all right, love, don't you worry,' said a voice, which seemed to come from far away.

She felt jolted and even sicker by the time she reached the district hospital. A nurse got her on to a bed in a cubicle and told her the doctor would be along to see her soon. The small room kept shifting around. Her mind began to drift. She remembered something awful had happened at Dance Club, but she could remember no details at all.

Annie was dimly conscious of someone looking at her head and asking her questions. When she opened her eyes next, her mum was sitting by the bed, holding her hand.

'Oh Mum, I must have dropped off to sleep,' she said in surprise.

'Are you all right, darling?' asked Mrs Macdonald, her brow furrowed with concern.

'Yes, I feel a bit better now. The giddiness seems to have gone off.'

A nurse came into the cubicle, with a porter. 'We're going to wheel her down to X-ray now, Mrs Macdonald. You can come too, if you like.'

When the X-rays revealed there was no fracture of the skull, the doctor said Annie would be able to go home the next morning.

'Oh can't I go now?' Annie complained. It was the first time she'd ever been in hospital and didn't fancy staying in overnight on her own.

'I think we'd better keep you in just for tonight,' the doctor answered, 'to keep an eye on you. You've had quite a knock to the head and a touch of concussion. That's what all the giddiness was about.'

'I've got to go now, pet,' said her mum, looking at her watch. 'Time to pick up Louisa. We'll be back later, though.'

Annie was moved to the children's ward, but didn't find anyone to talk to – the ward seemed to be full of babies and toddlers. When tea was brought round, she couldn't face it. She sat in bed, brooding until her parents returned; she knew something had gone badly wrong at Dance Club – would it mean the end of the club?

She was pleased to see her parents at visiting time, though she quickly began to wish her dad would go away again. His concern showed itself as anger against the Dance Club.

'If you hadn't started it up this would never have happened!' he said.

'Oh Dad,' said Annie. 'It could have happened anywhere!'

'I'd like to get to the bottom of what was going on in that club of yours!' he went on.

'Well it's no use asking me,' said Annie, rather sulkily, 'I can't remember a thing.'

'Don't go on at her, love,' said her mum.

'Sorry,' said her dad, 'but just promise me there'll be no dancing of any description for a week – to give yourself time to recover properly.'

Annie reluctantly gave her promise, while her mum went off to fetch Louisa in from the corridor. (Only two visitors per patient were allowed.)

'I'll say goodbye now,' her dad said, standing up.

Annie looked down the ward and to her amazement, saw Cherry walking beside her sister, carrying a bunch of flowers.

'Cherry!' she called out. 'What are you doing here?'

'Visiting the wounded,' said Cherry, with a grin.

'How's your head?'

Annie touched it and winced. There was a large egg-like swelling now where she had banged it.

'Ooh, that's a big lump!' cried Louisa, plonking herself on to the bed, to get a closer look.

'Ouch, mind where you're sitting!' Annie yelled. 'That was my leg!'

'Oh sorry,' said Louisa, unabashed. 'How did you manage to do it, anyway?'

'I don't really know,' said Annie. 'I just remember an awful row, then everything went black.'

'It was all Wayne and Darren's fault,' Cherry said.

'Oh I'd forgotten they were there,' said Annie.

'There was a *huge* fight, and you got your head cracked against the wall, just as Mrs Race walked in.'

Annie's eyes opened wide. 'I knew something terrible had happened. Don't tell me – Dance Club has been banned!'

'I think it came pretty close,' Cherry replied. 'Mr Reynolds was *furious!*'

'Oh no! Did it get reported to him?' Annie cried.

'Mrs Race said she *had* to report it because of your injury and everything.'

'What did he say?' asked Annie.

'Well,' said Cherry. 'What *didn't* he say!'

'Come on, Cherry, what about the club?'

'We can carry on, don't worry, but he stressed it was our VERY LAST CHANCE. If there is so much of a hint of bad behaviour ever again, that's it. End of club.'

'You'll have to be very good,' Louisa piped up.

Cherry laughed. 'We will, won't we? When are you coming out, Annie?'

'Tomorrow. I expect I'll have the day at home and get back to school on Thursday.'

'That's good,' said Cherry. 'We need you back to teach us the Magic Toyshop dances.'

Annie shook her head.

'Don't you think you'll be up to it?' asked Cherry.

'Louisa,' said Annie suddenly. 'Could you go and ask a nurse for a vase of water for these flowers?'

'All right,' said Louisa, jumping up. As she disappeared from the ward, Cherry asked,

'Did you want to get rid of her or something?'

'Aye,' Annie replied. 'You see, Dad's made me promise not to dance for a week.'

'What!'

'It's bad enough having to miss my classes at Miss Rodelles, especially with the National exam so close, but Dance Club as well! We've just so little time to get ready for this show.'

'I know,' said Cherry, 'and you're the only one who knows what to teach.'

Annie sighed, and then a determined look came into her eyes. 'Blow it, I'm going to come. I just won't do any dancing myself.'

The girls grinned conspiratorially. 'But what about the extra rehearsal we'd arranged after school on Friday?' asked Cherry.

79

'I'll say I'm coming to your house,' said Annie.

By Thursday, Annie felt quite fit again, and determined to make Dance Club a success. Mrs Race had told Cherry and Pip to come and tell her immediately if Wayne and Darren gate-crashed again, and so the girls felt relieved on that score.

Sam looked relieved too. In fact the atmosphere at the club that day was wonderful. Everyone seemed to be pulling together now, united against the common enemy. Even Maria and Zoë were co-operative.

Friday's rehearsal was for the principals and soloists only, so they could start some of the more individual work. They decided to start with the 'Somewhere' duet from *West Side Story*.

'Shall I coach this?' Annie whispered to Pip. 'I know you'd be better at it, but it might be awkward for you.'

'No, I'd like to do it,' said Pip.

It was obvious from the beginning of the rehearsal that Maria was going to resent whatever Pip said to her, even though her suggestions were helpful and imaginative. Sam, on the other hand, took on board everything Pip said to him. His performance improved dramatically during the rehearsal.

Maria struck a flat note, and Pip played it on the piano, to emphasize the fact.

'You're not getting the top A, Maria,' she pointed out. 'Let's have the last few bars again, shall we?'

Maria flung her arms up in the air. 'I can't stand this!' she yelled. 'Who does she think she is, telling *me* I'm flat!'

'Calm down, Maria,' Annie intervened. '*Someone's* got to coach you.'

'But not *her*,' said Maria. 'She hasn't a clue.'

'She's the only singer amongst us,' said Annie, 'as you well know.'

'And she sings in tune,' Cherry added, with a twinkle of mischief in her eye.

'What d'you mean by that?' Maria shouted.

'Sh, sh,' Annie pleaded. 'We can't have anyone yelling. Please, Maria, just do as Pip wants you to.'

'I've had enough for today,' said Maria. 'I've got a headache.'

'Fine,' said Annie, 'we'll get on with something else. How about your Christmas angel solo, Cherry?'

Maria flounced out of the drama room, as Annie started showing Cherry the opening steps of her dance.

'Phew,' said Pip. 'This isn't going to be easy.'

'We never thought it would be,' said Cherry.

'The duet's coming on well, though,' said Annie brightly. 'We'll get there in the end.'

Annie spent a quiet weekend at home, missing her dance classes with Miss Rodelle. As soon as she went into school on Monday morning, however, she could sense something had happened. There was an excited buzz in the schoolyard.

She quickly found Pip and Cherry. 'What's going on?' she asked.

'Haven't you heard?' said Cherry. 'The school's been burgled.'

'Has much been stolen?'

'Not all that much,' said Pip. 'The best computer and printer from the IT room.'

'And lots of software,' added Cherry.

'I wonder if they pinched any of those new keyboards from the music department?' said Annie.

It turned out that the music block had been left undisturbed. In fact, there was no sign of a forced entry in the main school either. Nothing other than the computer equipment had been stolen, but even this loss was a serious blow for the school.

'It was very expensive equipment,' Mrs Clanger explained to them, in form-time, 'and the insurance won't pay up for some time, so they won't be replaced in a hurry, I'm afraid.'

'When do the police think the burglary happened?' Annie asked her.

'The caretaker discovered the computer had gone missing on Friday evening, so they think it must have been taken late Friday afternoon,' said Mrs Clanger.

There was another shock for the children when they went to their information technology lesson later in the morning. Their teacher, Mr Cunningham, told them that the whole class's work – on disk – had been stolen along with the computer, which meant they would have to start their projects again from scratch.

To add insult to injury, all the games in the room had been stolen too. Mr Cunningham often let them spend the last ten minutes of their lesson with him playing on one or other of the computer games.

'If burglars only realized the upset they caused!' Annie exclaimed to her friends after the lesson.

At lunch-time a message came from Mr Reynolds requesting the three of them to go to his office as soon as possible.

'Oh no,' Cherry moaned, 'he's going to go on at us *again* about last week.'

'I can't imagine what he can say that he hasn't already said,' said Pip.

When they walked into his office, Annie was taken aback to see a young constable with him.

'This is PC Whiting,' said Mr Reynolds, answering their puzzled expressions. 'He wants to ask you a few questions in connection with the burglary on Friday.'

'I believe you three were on the premises last Friday afternoon after school,' said the young detective.

'That's right,' said Cherry. 'We were rehearsing for our dance show. We're running a club and ...'

'Yes, thank you, Cherry,' Mr Reynolds interrupted. 'The officer knows all about that already.'

'What time did your rehearsal begin?' asked PC Whiting, jotting down notes in his pocket book.

'Straight after school,' said Annie. 'About four.'

'And what time did it finish?'

'Five o'clock. I caught the 5.05 bus home.'

'Could you give me the names of those of you who were at the rehearsal?' he asked.

'The three of us,' Annie answered, 'Sam Murray, Kim and Susie Dorricott and Maria Farran.'

'And all of you stayed in the drama room the whole time, until five o'clock?'

'Yes,' said Annie.

'No,' said Pip. 'Don't forget Maria left early.'

'That's Maria Farran? Why did she leave early?'

Annie exchanged glances with Pip. She didn't want Mr Reynolds to get any hint of quarrelling between members of the club.

'Oh, we'd finished rehearsing her bit first,' Annie explained.

'Now, think carefully, did any of you hear or see anything unusual while you were in the drama room, or when you were on your way out of school at the end? You see, you were the only people left in the building. All the staff had left by 4.30 and the caretaker was having tea in his house between 4.45 and 5. When he came back to lock up just after that, the burglary had taken place. So you were the only ones in school when it happened.'

This came as quite a shock. Annie shook her head. 'Everything seemed quite normal,' she said.

'There was no forced entry,' said the police constable, 'and the only entrance left open was the one which led to the drama and IT block. To get to the IT room, the burglars would have had to pass the room in which you were rehearsing.'

'As the officer has discovered for himself, the room has a glazed door and several windows overlooking the passageway,' added the head-teacher. 'It is impossible to believe that not one of you saw the intruders walk past!'

'Of course, we haven't questioned your other friends yet,' said PC Whiting quickly, looking a bit uncomfortable at the heavy-handed tone Mr Reynolds had taken. 'Perhaps one of them saw something, but thought nothing of it. That often happens, of course.'

'Are you *absolutely* sure you saw no one go past?' asked Mr Reynolds, with a strong note of suspicion in his voice.

'Quite sure,' the three girls said.

'And none of you left the room apart from Maria?'

'No,' Annie replied. 'The rest of us were there until five.'

She was feeling very uncomfortable. Her palms and her nose were beginning to sweat, her cheeks felt hot and her breathing felt tight and shallow. She was beginning to pick up a strong feeling that Mr Reynolds suspected that she and her friends had something to do with this burglary. Unbelievable though it was, Annie could see that the timing of their rehearsal was going to keep them under the shadow of suspicion until the real culprits were caught.

The girls couldn't get out of the office fast enough, and positively flew to the relative safety of their music lesson. At least there everything seemed normal.

In the next break, they just had time to warn Sam that the police would want to ask him some questions, before the summons came to Mr Reynolds' office.

'I hope old Reynolds doesn't go on at him like he did at us,' said Pip. 'Sam's upset enough as it is.'

'Is he?' asked Annie.

'Wayne and Darren are still following him around and bullying him, I think,' said Pip. 'Not that he'll tell you much about it.'

'It must be awful for him,' said Annie.

'It's all very mysterious, this burglary,' said Cherry. 'I wonder how they *did* get in without any of us seeing?'

'Goodness knows,' said Annie, 'but life is going to be pretty uncomfortable for us until the crime is solved.'

'D'you think Mr Reynolds thinks we did it?' asked Pip.

'Either us, or someone we're in league with,' said Annie. 'I can't believe it.'

The faces of her two friends reflected Annie's sentiments.

'What can we do?' cried Pip.

'We can hope the police solve it quickly,' said Annie. 'Or else …'

'Or else what?' asked Cherry.

'Or else, we do a little detective work ourselves!'

· 8 ·

Row on the River-bank

Mrs Race had a conference with the three friends the next day after netball.

'I'm afraid Mr Reynolds is getting very cold feet about your Dance Club,' she said.

'We know,' said Cherry. 'And now we think he suspects us of having something to do with the school burglary!'

'Oh I'm sure he thinks no such thing,' said Mrs Race, 'but he has been threatening to call off your show.'

'Oh I hope he doesn't!' cried Annie.

'It's touch and go,' said Mrs Race. 'But look, I'll go and speak to him later. See what I can do.'

'Thank you, Mrs Race!' they all cried.

She laughed. 'I shouldn't thank me yet. I might not be able to do anything.'

When they were getting changed, the girls agreed that Mrs Race was without doubt the nicest teacher in the school.

'What if she doesn't persuade him?' said Pip.

'She must!' said Annie fiercely. 'I can't bear all our work to go for nothing.'

Inwardly, though, she felt very anxious.

The morning seemed to drag by. History had never seemed so dull. Even the marvels of the tomb of Tutankhamun failed to interest Annie. And in English, Mrs Clanger's silly jokes seemed even sillier than usual. Annie normally enjoyed both history and English a great deal, especially when she was called upon to write essays or stories. She was a capable writer – her father always said she took after him. He loved nothing more than when she came top in English. Annie knew he would be delighted if she were to go on to university to read an English degree.

Thinking about her dad brought on another worry. So far he hadn't found out that she had broken her promise to him, but now there was all this fuss about the burglary, he might.

'I hope Mr Reynolds doesn't ring up our parents,' she said to her friends at break.

'Or the police,' said Pip in a frightened squeak.

'Well, neither of them have yet,' said Cherry in a matter-of-fact tone, 'so I don't suppose they will.'

'It would be dreadful if Dad found out I'd been to Dance Club after promising I wouldn't.'

'We'll keep our fingers crossed for you,' said Pip.

'I wonder if Mrs Race has seen the head yet,' said Cherry.

'If only this stupid burglary hadn't happened!' cried Annie. 'It's made everything ten times worse for us.'

'It's so puzzling,' said Pip. 'I mean, if the burglars came into school when we were there, why didn't we see or hear them?'

'Unless they were already inside the school,' said Annie. 'Then they could have slipped out just after we did.'

'I suppose you can see why Mr Reynolds suspects it's someone on the inside,' sighed Cherry.

'What about Maria?' Annie said suddenly, keeping her voice low so it wouldn't carry across the school yard, at the other side of which Maria was standing with Zoë.

'Annie!' said Cherry, pretending to look shocked. 'You were the one who thought Maria was OK up till now. What's happened?'

'I don't know,' said Annie. 'It must be all these suspicions flying around. I can't *really* imagine her stealing a computer.'

'She did have the opportunity, though,' said Pip.

'It's a mystery,' said Annie. 'And *somebody* certainly did it.'

Pip suddenly went white.

'What's the matter?' asked Annie. 'Have you

89

guessed who the culprit is?'

'No,' said Pip. 'What day is it?'

'Tuesday,' said Cherry. 'Why?'

'Oh stinking cabbage leaves!' yelled Pip, looking at her watch. 'I'm supposed to be at my clarinet lesson!'

'You'd better get moving then,' said Cherry.

'It's no use,' wailed Pip. 'I've forgotten to bring my clarinet to school. Miss Stevens will kill me!'

Miss Stevens was one of the visiting wind instrumental teachers. She had a reputation which made most of her pupils very wary of her.

'Best thing you can do is to go and see her straight away and apologize,' said Cherry firmly.

'Couldn't you go and tell her I've got a headache, or something,' Pip wailed.

'She'll see through it straight away,' said Cherry. 'Just tell her the truth. It's always best in the long run.'

Pip gathered her strength for the ordeal that faced her and sprinted off to find Miss Stevens.

'Typical Pip!' said Cherry. 'I hope she doesn't get into too much trouble!'

The next two lessons – double chemistry – seemed to go by more slowly than the first three. Pip came in late, after being held up by a ticking-off from Miss Stevens. She told Annie and Cherry that she'd been warned that if it happened again she wouldn't be allowed to continue her lessons.

At last it was lunch-time. Annie had a pang of

90

guilt about her father, as she walked into the gym with her friends. But the Dance Club was so exciting, especially now the show rehearsals were under way.

When everyone had assembled, Cherry asked Annie quietly if they'd better say something about Mr Reynolds threatening to close the club.

'I don't think we should,' Annie whispered back. 'Let's look on the bright side. We don't want to alarm everyone for nothing.'

'But Annie,' Pip started.

'No,' said Annie. 'Let's get on with the rehearsal.'

Pip and Cherry had come up with some ideas for the Jets and Sharks dance from *West Side Story* that they wanted to try out. For the first time since her accident, Annie found herself actually dancing. It felt great.

Pip and Cherry divided the club into two groups, to represent the two rival gangs.

'I'm really pleased we're doing this dance,' Robbie said to them.

'Me too,' said Sam. 'I just love the music.'

The girls had worked out appropriately spiky movements for the spiky phrases of music and even managed to let the able dancers do some more complicated bits without the 'ducklings' seeming to be left out of it.

'I really like what you've choreographed so far,' Annie said to her friends at the end. 'Well done.'

'If only we get to do this show,' said Pip.

'We've just got to keep working,' said Annie. 'If

we believe hard enough there'll be a show, there'll be a show!'

Cherry giggled at her friend's fierceness. Sometimes Annie seemed an unstoppable force.

The friends called some of the members together to arrange an after-school rehearsal the following evening.

'Can you make that, Maria?' asked Annie.

'Are we doing 'Somewhere' again?' Maria asked, tossing her long black plait over her shoulder.

Annie nodded.

'Good,' said Maria. 'I've worked out some different movements during the song for me and Sam.'

Annie's mouth dropped open. 'But we've already practised it the way Pip's choreographed it!' she protested.

'Wait and see mine,' said Maria, moving away. 'It's much better.'

'Oh that girl's impossible,' said Cherry.

'I don't mind if she wants to change it,' said Pip. '*She*'s singing it.'

'It's the way she goes about everything,' said Annie. 'Oh well, you did warn me.'

There was still no word from Mrs Race when the club principals met again the next day after school.

'Perhaps she hasn't been able to catch Mr Reynolds,' Cherry suggested.

'You don't think she'd have forgotten?' said Pip.

'Nay, I'm sure not,' Annie replied. 'I wonder if she's having a real struggle to persuade him to keep the club open?'

As she finished speaking, Annie was aware, too late, that Maria had come up behind them and had overheard what she'd said.

'You haven't told the rest of us there's a problem,' Maria said accusingly.

'We didn't want to worry …'

'So the club's days are numbered,' Maria cut in.

'No, it's not like that at all,' said Annie, feeling exasperated. 'Mrs Race is on our side. I'm sure she'll be able to shake Mr Reynolds out of his doubts.'

'I don't like the way you haven't been honest with us,' Maria snapped. 'Not at all.'

Annie saw that the only way to get out of a row was to ask Maria to show them the work she'd done on 'Somewhere'. Maria was only too keen. She taught Sam the new movements as they went along.

Pip's more subtle movements had disappeared, replaced by ones that were over-dramatic, embarrassing even. Poor Sam looked most uncomfortable throughout the duet. He looked pleadingly at Annie every time he caught her eye. Annie knew she mustn't trigger another row with Maria. But she couldn't leave the duet looking like that!

'What d'you think?' Maria cried at the end.

'I don't know,' said Cherry, hedging. 'It's difficult to judge when you're still showing it to Sam.'

'I can't really say,' said Pip helplessly. 'I'm so used to my own choreography now!'

Everyone looked expectantly at Annie.

Annie chose her words carefully. 'I – um – liked most of your ideas – in principle,' she said, 'but I do think we need to tone it all down a little.'

'Tone it down?'

'It'll be easy,' said Annie in her most diplomatic tone. 'We'll leave it for next time. Just a slight change in emphasis. Yes, thanks, Maria. Can we have a look at your Spanish solo, now?'

By the end of the meeting, Annie felt tired out with being tactful. She knew now what directors had to suffer when dealing with temperamental 'artistes'. Fortunately, Maria left the drama room first, so the remaining friends – Sam included – could have a good moan about her.

They wandered out of school by the back entrance. It was a fine autumn afternoon and they thought it would be pleasant to walk into town along by the river. As they crunched through piles of leaves down the lawns towards the river-bank, they could see a team of older Bishops' boys and girls, practising their rowing on the river.

'That looks fun,' said Annie. 'When do we get a chance?'

'Not till Year 11 or 12,' said Cherry. 'I can't wait!'

'I'd be no good,' said Pip.

'Why not?' asked Sam.

'I'd probably lose the oar in the water!'

'Course you wouldn't,' said Sam. 'You can come with me. I'd look after you.'

'Those two seem to be getting on well,' Cherry whispered to Annie. But Annie hadn't noticed –

she was too deep in thought about Mr Reynolds and the Dance Club.

A shadow ahead made her look up in surprise. Progress forward was blocked by Wayne and Darren.

'What have we here?' said Wayne gleefully.

'Four sweet little dancers,' said Darren in a sugary voice.

'What are you hanging about here for?' Annie asked, determined not to let her fear show.

'Hanging about? We're not hanging about, are we, Wayne? No, we've got a reason to be here all right!'

'And what reason's that?' Annie demanded. 'Don't tell me they've let you in the rowing team!'

A flicker of anger passed across Darren's eyes, as Annie's friends giggled.

'It's little Nooryef we've got business with,' he said sharply. 'You girls can mess off.'

Pip took a protective step closer to Sam. Annie and Cherry stood their ground in front of them. But in a flash, Wayne, the bigger boy, had darted round them, caught hold of Sam's arm and pulled him over. Sam immediately curled up on the ground, his arms protecting his head.

'Don't you touch him!' yelled Pip.

Wayne stepped back and hesitated. This gave Sam the opportunity to jump up and run back in the direction of school. Wayne made a move after him, but Darren held him back.

'Better not follow him in there,' he growled.

By this time, Annie's temper was flaming.

'You pair of cowards!' she yelled. 'Why don't you leave Sam alone?'

The boys chuckled and sauntered back along the river.

'You stupid idiots!' she shouted after them. 'Big bullies! I hate you!' she shouted, even louder, as they moved further away.

As she drew breath for another good yell, Cherry elbowed her fiercely in the ribs, making her gasp instead.

'Wha-at?' she said, indignantly. Cherry inclined her head towards school. Annie swivelled round and saw Mr Reynolds bearing down on them. He looked furious. Annie's heart sank into her boots.

'Was that you shouting, Annie Macdonald?' he demanded. 'Perhaps you can explain why you are creating a disturbance on school premises at this hour!'

Annie opened her mouth to explain, but Mr Reynolds didn't give her chance.

'This unseemly behaviour is beyond me. Perhaps it was acceptable in Scotland! But it is certainly *not acceptable* here!' He looked at his watch, and Annie grabbed her chance to speak.

'You see, Wayne and Darren … ' she began.

'I suppose you've just finished one of your extra Dance Club meetings,' Mr Reynolds interrupted. 'You can take a detention for this episode, Annie. Now, the three of you, get on your way home. Without causing any more disturbances!'

Before Annie could say another word, he turned his back on them and stalked back to school.

'Wow!' said Pip. 'He was cross.'

'It's so unfair!' wailed Annie. 'He didn't give me a chance to explain at all.'

Cherry put her arm round her friend. 'And somehow I think our chances of keeping the Dance Club open have taken a nose-dive.'

Tap Shoes

Thursday morning passed without any further
word from Mr Reynolds, which gave Annie a little
room for hope. At their Dance Club session that
day, the girls planned to start the tap sequence for
the show. They had to exclude the 'ducklings', who
had had no tap training, but they all wanted to
come and watch.

Robbie, however, begged to be allowed to join in.

'If I don't pick it up quickly, I promise I'll drop
out,' he said.

'I don't know,' Annie said doubtfully, but then he
gave her one of his quick, shy smiles. 'Oh well, all
right.' She had certainly been impressed by the easy

way he had picked up the Modern and ballet movements.

'Hang on a minute,' said Pip, who was to be in charge of the tap session. 'He can't tap without tap shoes.'

'That's quickly solved,' said Sam with a grin. 'I've got a spare pair kicking around school. I'll go and get them.'

'But Robbie's a lot taller than you,' said Annie.

'We're the same shoe size,' Robbie explained. 'Sam's got big feet for his height!'

'You mean you've got small ones!' yelled Sam over his shoulder.

Pip started teaching the group of students. She'd chosen a piece of music that wouldn't be too fast – 'Spread a Little Happiness' – so that there was more chance of getting the dance polished.

Sam returned with a puzzled expression.

'Can't find them,' he said. 'Could have sworn I left them in my locker. Sorry, Robbie.'

Annie felt quite sorry for Robbie – he looked so disappointed. The girls promised they would dig about in the lost property box at Miss Rodelle's and see if they could find a pair of tap shoes his size.

His face lit up again. 'Thanks! That would be great!'

Before they could start their tap work again, Mrs Race strode into the gym.

'I think you should all hear this,' she said.

The club members gathered around her.

'This looks like bad news to me,' said Pip.

'Sh,' said Annie, listening intently. Mrs Race had started telling everyone about Mr Reynolds' feelings towards the club.

'The headteacher,' said Mrs Race, 'is very concerned about the risks of having unsupervised club meetings. As you know, I'm just too busy to take you on and there is no one else interested, I'm afraid.'

'So is he closing the club?' asked Annie, unable to contain herself.

'I'm afraid so,' Mrs Race answered.

There were moans and groans all round.

'But what about our show?' asked Annie, feeling angry tears welling up into her eyes.

'Well there I think I've done you a bit of good,' Mrs Race said. 'I put it to the headteacher that the whole concert would have to be cancelled if you weren't allowed to do your part, so he agreed you could still do that. You can continue with your lunch-time rehearsals until the concert. But he was adamant, no more after-school rehearsals.' She shrugged her shoulders. 'He seems to have set his mind against the Dance Club continuing after that.'

Mrs Race looked genuinely sorry for the disappointment her news was causing among the children.

'I'm very sorry,' she said. 'But it's not a good time just now, with the upset of the burglary and everything.'

The girls went off to their afternoon lessons in very low spirits.

'Just our luck,' said Pip.

'I mean, we've only just started!' said Cherry.

'Well, at least we get to do the show,' said Annie, trying to sound at least slightly cheerful.

'But when you know there's no future and you're not building up to bigger and better things ...' began Pip. She didn't finish her sentence, but her friends knew exactly what she meant. It *was* very disappointing.

'And another thing,' cried Cherry. 'We'll never get everything together in time just with the lunch-time meetings!'

'I'd been thinking about that,' said Annie. 'We'll have to meet at each other's houses – just the principals, I mean.'

'I live much too far out to offer,' Pip said quickly.

Cherry was nodding. 'The Vicarage would be perfect. I'm sure Mum and Dad wouldn't mind. We could use the big dining room – it's hardly ever used by the family!'

'Great!' said Annie. 'Ask them tonight.'

Annie tried hard to take her mind off the problems of the Dance Club by concentrating on the slippery wet clay she was moulding in her hands. The pottery teacher had told them all to make a face in relief with a flat back, which they would be able to paint and glaze another time.

When Annie found she hadn't enough clay to finish hers, she went across to the corner of the room, to fetch an extra lump.

The pottery room was in a basement of the oldest

part of the Bishops' School buildings. It was quite small, which meant classes always had to be split between pottery and painting, but very inviting. There were clay pots and models everywhere waiting to be glazed or fired. The kiln was in a small adjoining room. Annie usually found the atmosphere relaxing and creative.

She found she had to open a new big bag of clay. Cutting open the strong polythene bag carefully, she peeled back the protective wrapping and was just about to scoop a handful of clay from the top, when something made her stop in her tracks.

Embedded in the surface of the clay was a footprint. She stared at it as the seconds ticked by. What could it mean?

Quietly, she called Pip and Cherry over to look.

'Strange place for a footprint, isn't it?' said Cherry. 'Why should anyone be walking about on the table in the pottery room?'

'Exactly,' said Annie. 'It's suspicious. Especially when you notice the position of the bag of clay.'

She looked upwards and her friends followed the direction of her gaze. Overhead was the basement window, which was actually at ground-level outside.

Cherry sucked in her breath. 'Oh I see what you're getting at now.'

'I don't,' Pip admitted.

'The burglary,' hissed Annie, putting her finger to her lips when she saw the pottery teacher approaching.

While her friends were still taking this in, Annie asked the teacher for permission to fetch Mr Reynolds, to show him the footprint in the clay.

The astonished teacher agreed, once Annie explained its significance to her, and Annie was allowed to go on her errand. Mr Reynolds looked even more surprised than the pottery teacher when Annie told him the reason for her visit. At first she could tell he thought she was making it up, but after a good many suspicious questions, he agreed to come with her.

'I'll inform the police about this,' he told them gravely after he'd inspected the clay. 'They'll decide whether it has any importance. Meanwhile, I'll have the caretaker take this bag to my study, to make sure it isn't tampered with.'

'He could have thanked me!' Annie complained later. 'No – he just stared at me as meanly as ever over those horrible spectacles of his!'

'Perhaps the police will decide it's an important clue,' said Cherry soothingly. 'Then he might be more grateful.'

'He probably thinks we stuck a shoe in it ourselves,' said Pip miserably, 'to lay a false trail.'

'I hadn't thought of that,' said Annie. She wished Pip hadn't either.

'It wasn't a very big footprint, was it?' said Cherry.

'No, and there weren't any patterns on it, like on a trainer sole,' Annie replied thoughtfully. 'More like a plain-soled girl's shoe, really.'

'What are you getting at?'

'I guess I'm just wondering about Maria again.'

'Well she couldn't have done it on her own,' said Pip.

'Where there's Maria, Zoë's never far behind,' said Annie.

'But why should they want to steal the computer, Annie?' Cherry protested.

Annie shrugged. 'People have all sorts of reasons for doing things.'

'I'm sure it must have been burglars who have nothing to do with the school,' said Cherry. 'I mean, now we know they got in through the pottery room, they could have got to the IT room without passing us in the drama room.'

'But the window isn't broken!' Pip pointed out, looking up.

'Let's have a closer look, shall we?' said Annie. She glanced across the classroom. The pottery teacher had taken a load of models to the kiln for firing.

Annie quickly stepped up on to the table where the bag of clay had stood and examined the window.

'The catch is broken,' she hissed. 'It would be fairly easy to lift up from outside.'

As she jumped down again, Cherry said, 'there you are then – point of entry.'

'But how would a burglar know that the catch was broken?' said Annie. 'The mystery deepens!'

The friends heard later that the police had been

in during the afternoon to examine the footprint in the clay, and the pottery room.

'Maybe they'll find some fingerprints too,' said Annie. 'I do hope they hurry up and catch the real culprits. Mr Reynolds might start being a bit nicer to us then!'

That evening, to Annie's relief, she was allowed to go back to her classes at Miss Rodelle's.

'I am glad to see you back,' said her teacher. 'I was beginning to worry we'd have to pull you out of the silver medal.'

'Don't worry,' said Annie. 'I've been practising at home.'

Miss Rodelle was very pleased with the Scottish National dance, after Annie had run through it.

'That's excellent,' she said.

'It's my favourite,' said Annie.

'It shows,' said Miss Rodelle. 'Just try now to get your other studies up to the same standard!'

Annie had a ballet class, too, after the National. By the time she got home, there wasn't much time left for her homework, so she got down to it straight away. She was still sitting in her bedroom putting the finishing touches to a map of France when the doorbell rang.

'Who can that be at this time of night?' she heard her father say, as he went to the front door.

There was a muffled conversation and then, to her surprise, her father called her down.

'Annie,' he said, when she'd come into the sitting room to find a policeman standing there – the constable who had asked her questions at school. 'This is Constable Whiting. He says he's come round to take a statement from you in connection with the school burglary.'

'Oh,' said Annie.

Her father and mother both looked worried and puzzled.

'Yes, that's right,' said the officer, taking out some forms and a notebook. 'There are two particular times I want to ask you about – the first is the actual evening of the burglary – the second is just yesterday – the circumstances in which you found the er – footprint in the clay.'

'Is it really necessary for my daughter to make a statement?' asked Mr Macdonald. 'I mean, there are plenty of other pupils at Bishop's School who must know just as much as she does about it, which is very little, I imagine.'

'Well, sir,' said the officer. 'Your daughter here was the person who found the – er – footprint in the clay and reported it to the headteacher.'

'Oh, I see,' said Mr Macdonald.

'Shall we do that part first?' suggested PC Whiting.

'OK,' said Annie nervously. It wasn't that part she was worried about. What she wasn't looking forward to was answering questions about the evening of the burglary, when, her Dad believed, she had been at Cherry's house.

After the officer was satisfied with the details of the finding of the footprint, Annie asked him, more as a delaying tactic than anything else, 'Did you find the broken window catch above the clay table?'

'Yes, thank you,' said PC Whiting. 'We did. We're pretty sure this is how the intruders got in.'

Annie didn't dare look at her father, in case he was already beginning to put two and two together.

'Funny thing about that print though,' the policeman went on, 'it was very likely made by a dancer.'

'A dancer!' exclaimed Annie. 'What makes you say that?'

'Our experts reckon it's the print of a tap-dancing shoe,' said PC Whiting staring hard at Annie. 'Bizarre, isn't it? Now we're looking for a tap-dancing burglar!' He chuckled, but his eyes didn't move from Annie's face. She felt horribly uncomfortable.

Any moment now it was going to come out that she'd been at Dance Club when she shouldn't have been. She could kick herself now for trying to deceive her parents. And, even worse, PC Whiting obviously suspected the Dance Club were involved in the burglary.

At last the dreaded question came: 'Could you tell me the exact times you started and finished at your Dance Club last Friday evening and which way you left the school?'

'Oh I think there's been some mistake,' said Mr Macdonald. 'You see, Annie didn't go to Dance Club that night. She'd had a bad bump on the head

108

a few days before …

'I don't think there's any mistake,' said the officer, leafing through his notebook. 'I've already asked your daughter about the evening in question. Yes, here we are. She told me that she was at the club on Friday.'

Annie looked at her shoes miserably. Her father made no more interruptions, but as she made her statement, she could sense he was dying to ask her a good many questions of his own. Her mother had gone very quiet.

At last the door was closed behind PC Whiting and Annie was left alone with her mum and dad.

'Now, young lady,' said her father, turning on her. 'We'd like a few explanations!'

· 10 ·

Rehearsing at Cherry's

The three friends had lots to talk about the next morning before lessons. Pip and Cherry were sympathetic as Annie described how furious her father had been with her. Of course, it had made it even worse when Annie had had to tell her parents she'd been given a detention, and why.

'You're certainly not having much luck!' exclaimed Cherry. 'Poor you!'

'I've never had a detention before,' said Annie. 'What's it like?'

'I've never had one either,' said Cherry.

'I have,' said Pip, 'for forgetting my games kit so many times. It's not half so bad as the thought of it, honestly. And you get a quiet hour to do your homework in.'

This made Annie feel a little better. 'Oh, I forgot to tell you the really important bit,' she said suddenly.

But just then Mrs Clanger came in to take the register and their conversation had to wait until they were moving down the corridor to their first lesson.

'The footprint in the clay,' Annie said to them then. 'That policeman said it was a *tap shoe* print! Can you believe it?'

'That's really odd,' said Cherry.

'A bit creepy,' said Pip, 'when you think how it links the burglary with the Dance Club.'

'I gave it a lot of thought in bed last night,' said Annie, 'and I reached the conclusion that either it was Maria, or someone who wanted it blamed on us.'

'You mean, we've been framed?' said Cherry.

'It's possible,' said Annie.

The girls had a busy day at school, with choir practice all through their lunch-hour, and had little more opportunity to chat. By the time Annie had finished her detention and walked into the centre of Shrewsbury, she was half an hour late for her Friday ballet class.

She apologized quickly to Miss Rodelle, bobbing a curtsey as she passed her, and fell into the back line of the Pre-elementary students.

As she began the set pieces in the centre, all her

112

problems and anxieties seemed to drop away from her. They were doing a sequence of chassés into arabesques, using the different arm positions. Annie put all her concentration into accurate positions of the feet, stretched toes, and graceful arms and hands.

It was heaven to dance without responsibility for anyone but herself. She loved running the Dance Club, but it was certainly causing her a lot of headaches at the moment. Annie felt glad she had the ability to 'switch off' when she was dancing. It was probably the reason she loved it so much.

Miss Rodelle seemed particularly pleased with her work that afternoon, and Annie went out into the changing room, feeling that life wasn't that bad, after all.

Pip, who had come in while she and Cherry were in ballet, was rummaging around in the large lost-property box.

'What are you doing?' Cherry asked her.

'Looking for tap shoes for Robbie,' said Pip. 'As promised.'

Annie and Cherry joined her and, after emptying the box, they found what they were looking for, right at the bottom.

'They're the right size, I think,' said Annie. 'They're a bit shabby, but I don't think he'll mind.'

'He's very keen,' said Cherry, looking at her in rather a sly way.

'I know,' said Annie. 'He's a natural dancer, isn't he? The way he picks everything up!'

'I didn't just mean keen on *dancing*,' said Cherry, with a giggle.

Annie felt her cheeks going pink. 'I don't know what you're on about, Cherry!'

'We'll believe you, thousands wouldn't,' Cherry giggled.

'Oh, leave her alone,' said Pip.

Annie felt a strong desire to change the subject. 'Did you manage to ask your parents about having rehearsals at your place?'

'Yes,' said Cherry, 'and they said they didn't mind at all. As long as it was no more than twice a week.'

'That should be enough,' said Annie. 'It'll make a lot of difference to us. Shall we fix up a couple of rehearsals for next week, then? Time's getting quite short now.'

'Don't remind me,' said Pip, glumly. 'After the show, no more club.'

'Don't think about it!' said Annie.

Cherry's mum popped her head round the door. 'Ready?' she asked.

'Nearly,' said Cherry, flinging a long sloppy jumper over her ballet things, and scooping up her shoes, hairbrush and case. 'Bye, you two. See you here tomorrow!'

Pip and Annie went into the waiting-room and sipped hot chocolate. They had another half an hour to go before their National class. Just before it was time to go back into the studio, they both slipped their black calf-length character skirts over their leotards. The skirts were very full, and made from a heavy cotton, trimmed with stripes of purple and pink ribbon near the hem.

Annie couldn't resist doing a twirl, letting the skirt flare out around her. She stooped down to change her pink satin ballet shoes for the black canvas, cuban-heeled shoes they used for Character and National work.

'Are you getting nervous yet about the exam?' Pip asked, as she fastened her own ankle straps.

'I can't believe it's only next week,' Annie replied. 'We've had so much else to think about, haven't we?'

'You can say that again,' said Pip. 'I just hope nothing else goes wrong before the show!'

The following week, however was to bring further problems. During their first Dance Club meeting at Tuesday lunch-time, Maria and Zoë were already waiting in the gym when Annie and her friends arrived. Maria looked belligerent, and Annie greeted her warily.

'So it's all your fault the club's having to close,' Maria snapped, without so much as a 'hello'.

'Hang on a minute,' said Annie. 'No, it's not!'

''S not what we've heard,' said Zoë.

'Mr Reynolds caught you shouting outside school after Dance Club last week, didn't he?' Maria yelled.

'Keep your voice down, Maria,' Cherry pleaded. Other club members were trickling now into the

115

gym and were listening in to the conversation.

'Well, yes,' said Annie, 'but what he's most worried about is the burglary and ...'

'Rubbish!' shouted Maria. 'This is your doing, Annie Macdonald, or should I say, Blabbermouth!'

Annie went furiously red. 'Get out of here!' she said. She just couldn't take any more.

'I'm going, don't worry,' said Maria. 'Come on, Zoë. And we wouldn't come back if you got down on your bended knees.'

'Good riddance!' said Annie, trying very hard not to shout. At the back of her mind was the fear that one of the teachers might walk in.

Maria and Zoë banged the door behind them with a resounding smack. The room went very quiet, until Cherry started giggling.

'I don't know what you're laughing about,' said Annie with a frown. 'Are we going to have show now?'

'Maria just looks so funny when she's angry,' said Cherry. 'Those bushy black eyebrows meet over her nose!' She exploded once more into giggles.

The Dorricott twins came over to the friends. 'Don't worry, Annie,' said one of them. Annie still couldn't tell which one. 'We won't let you down. We'll stick with you till the show.'

'That's very helpful, thank you,' said Annie. It had indeed been a strong fear that other Wenlock dancers would follow Maria's example.

'Can we manage without Maria and Zoë?' Pip asked.

'Well, it certainly solves one problem,' said Annie, suddenly seeing the lighter side. 'We won't have to suffer her awful treatment of 'Somewhere'.'

'That'll be a great relief,' said Sam, who had joined the group.

'And you'll be able to do your part after all, Pip!' Annie exclaimed.

Pip started to grin. 'Can't be all bad then, can it?'

'What about the Spanish solo?' Cherry asked.

'We'll just have to cut it,' said Annie. 'It's a great pity, but still. And Zoë's only got a very small part – one of the 'ducklings' can step in.'

'Things might even be better,' said Cherry, 'without Maria and Zoë around.'

'You might be right,' said Annie, 'but Maria is such a good dancer. She'll be a real loss to us in that way.'

The following day did not allow Annie any time to brood over Maria leaving the Dance Club. Her National dance exam was scheduled for three o'clock and she spent all day anticipating it. She and Pip grew more and more nervous as the school day wore on. They had permission to leave Bishops' at two, which gave them plenty of time of catch a bus to Miss Rodelle's, where the examinations were taking place.

'Good luck!' Cherry called after them down the corridor.

'Thanks, we'll need it,' Annie called back. It had

117

been quite a time since she had taken a dancing exam. She had forgotten how nerve-racking they were.

Once at the studio, they had over half an hour to change and do their hair. It was vital to look impeccably neat and tidy. Every last wisp of hair was gelled and sprayed firmly back into a tight bun before Miss Rodelle was satisfied with them.

'Don't forget to smile at the examiner,' she said. 'Smile, smile, smile. Look as if you hadn't a care in the world.'

'It's difficult when your tummy's turning over and over,' groaned Pip.

'You'll be fine, don't worry,' the young teacher said. 'I have high hopes for both of you.'

The most frightening part of the exam for Annie was doing the set dances individually. The examiner – a middle-aged, pleasant-looking woman – returned her smiles, however, which put her more at ease. Once Annie was into the Scottish dance, which she knew so very well by now, she began to enjoy herself. The smile on her face felt more natural, and the elation of moving expertly flooded her whole body.

'Thank you,' said the examiner, at the end of her solo. Annie's eyes met hers for a moment, as she curtseyed her own thank you.

If only I could read her mind, she thought. *Have I won my silver medal*? She just hoped she wouldn't have to wait too long for the results.

Annie went to bed that night tired out, but

reasonably satisfied with the account she had given of herself in the exam. As soon as she woke, she was re-shaping the show in her head, to get round the loss of Maria and Zoë.

The club's first after-school meeting at Cherry's house was that afternoon. It proved a great success. Mrs Stevens had baked some delicious flapjack 'to keep them going', as she put it. And the rehearsal itself went really well.

Pip and Sam ran through the duet 'Somewhere', a couple of times, reinstating Pip's original movements.

'Right, now give it all you've got,' said Annie. 'Hang on, Cherry, go and fetch your mum. It'll be good for them to have an audience.'

'Oh no!' wailed Pip. 'It'll make me nervous.'

'You've got to get used to it,' said Annie. 'You'll soon be singing in front of a packed school hall.'

Pip went rather pale, but, once Mrs Stevens was installed at the back of the dining-room, managed to sing like an angel. She and Sam moved wonderfully together too.

'That was sensational!' cried Annie when they'd finished.

'It certainly was,' said Mrs Stevens. 'I had no idea you had such talent in your club! You couldn't bear to do it again, could you? I know Cherry's father would be spellbound!'

When Pip and Sam agreed, Mrs Stevens went off to fetch her husband and reappeared with him a few moments later. A huge barrel of a man, he had

119

a big bushy greying beard and sparkling eyes.

'I'm in for a treat, I hear,' he said, before making himself comfortable.

'I don't know about that,' said Sam, grinning nervously. 'I've never sung to a vicar before,' he whispered to Pip. Pip and Sam did their encore, and received a big round of applause from the Stevenses.

'Wow, I enjoyed that,' said Pip at the end. 'If only the Dance Club could always be like this.'

'You were terrific!' said Annie.

Pip's eyes were gleaming with pleasure and excitement. 'Oh no,' she said, looking at her watch, 'I haven't been watching the time. I've missed my bus!'

'Isn't there another one?' asked Cherry.

'Not for two and a half hours!' wailed Pip.'You know what these rural services are like.'

'Don't worry about it,' said Cherry. 'My dad'll run you home. No problem.'

'No, no,' said Pip, with great emphasis Annie thought. 'I couldn't possibly. Look, can I ring my parents? They'll have to come and fetch me.'

'Of course,' said Cherry. 'I'll show you the 'phone.'

Sam had already left when Cherry came back into the dining-room.

'She's having trouble getting through, I think,' said Cherry.

'She certainly didn't like the idea of your dad running her home, did she?' Annie commented.

'No,' said Cherry, 'but it's typical of Pip. She's very secretive in that way.'

'But what's she got to hide?' asked Annie.

'Goodness knows.'

'I wonder,' said Annie, rubbing her forehead, 'if her parents aren't very well off and they live in a little tumbledown cottage, or something? You know, perhaps she's *ashamed* for us to see her home.'

'What a pity if that's the reason,' said Cherry. 'I mean, it wouldn't bother us a bit, would it? Pip is still Pip, our friend.'

'I wish we could get it out into the open,' said Annie. 'It must make her feel bad.'

They stopped talking, as soon as Pip opened the door.

'Did you get through?' asked Cherry.

'Yes thanks,' said Pip. 'They said they'd meet me in half an hour.'

'They could pick you up here,' said Cherry.

'No, it's OK, I said I'll walk back towards the ring-road. It's easier for them.'

Annie and Cherry exchanged glances.

'Do you want us to walk with you?' asked Annie.

'No, no, really. I'm fine,' said Pip.

'Have you got to rush off, Annie?' asked Cherry.

'No,' said Annie. 'I can hang on a bit.'

'Good,' said Cherry. 'We can have a cosy chat – the three of us.'

Pip seemed to have become rather tense, and it took a while for her to relax. Annie brought up the subject of the burglary again.

'I think I know the reason no one saw the burglars taking the computer and stuff out on to the busy street in broad daylight.'

'Oh?' said Cherry. 'What is it?'

'Because they didn't,' said Annie.

'How d'you mean?' asked Pip.

'They didn't come out on to the street at all,' said Annie. 'If you think where the pottery room is – at the back of the school. The burglars, I reckon, got out that way too and made their way through the grounds to the river.'

'But it's a long way to walk along the river-bank, carrying a heavy computer and printer,' argued Cherry.

'I don't say they *walked*,' said Annie.

'Oh, I get it!' said Pip. 'They used a boat.'

'Exactly,' said Annie. 'Just a simple rowing boat would have done. There's plenty of them tied up all along the river's edge. Easy enough to borrow one.'

'Or nick one,' said Cherry. 'Or they could have used a school canoe!'

'I'd better start walking now,' said Pip, standing up. 'Thanks for everything, Cherry.'

'You sure you don't want us to walk with you?' Cherry asked.

'I'm sure,' said Pip. 'See you, Annie.'

Cherry showed her out and returned to Annie.

'I don't like to think of her walking about by herself now. It's going dark,' she said. 'I wish she'd let us go with her.'

122

'Well, why don't we go anyway?' suggested Annie. 'Follow at a discreet distance, like spies. It'd be fun. And we could keep an keep an eye on her. Make sure she meets her parents safely.'

Cherry didn't need asking twice. She had her coat on in an instant. As she and Annie let themselves out and set off quietly down the avenue, they could just see Pip's slight figure bobbing ahead in the distance.

'Should be pretty easy, in this twilight,' said Annie. 'But if she should look round, jump back behind a tree or something.'

'It's quite exciting, isn't it?' said Cherry, with a giggle.

They followed Pip through the estate which led to the big ring-road island. It was easy enough to find some cover behind a row of shops here, where they could look out. Pip was standing, waiting, at the island.

'I wonder why she wanted to go on her own,' mused Annie.

'I don't know,' said Cherry. 'It's as though she doesn't want us to see her parents. Hang on,' she hissed. 'There's a vehicle slowing up.'

'That can't be it!' said Annie. 'It's an old Rolls!'

'You're right!' squealed Cherry, open-mouthed. 'But it's definitely stopping.'

The gleaming silver Rolls-Royce had indeed come to a halt inches from Pip. They saw Pip bend forward to speak to the driver, but the friends couldn't see who this was. And then, before they could take it all in, Pip had got into the back seat, and the beautiful old car had driven off along the ring-road.

· 11 ·

A Figure in the Alley

'It's so frustrating not being able to ask her about it,' Annie said to Cherry before registration the next morning. Pip hadn't yet arrived.

'We couldn't possibly admit we were following her!' said Cherry. 'The only thing I can think is her father runs a wedding car firm or something.'

'Yet another unsolved mystery,' Annie sighed. 'I wonder if the police are any closer to finding the burglars?'

'I expect we'll be the last to know when they do,' said Cherry.

'Anyway, we've got to put our minds to this show,' said Annie. 'We've got ten days exactly, and we haven't even started thinking about costumes yet!'

'Let's discuss them at the club at lunch-time,' said Cherry.

Annie took up her friend's suggestion. Over half the meeting time was taken up with sorting out what everyone would need to wear.

'Are the T-shirts going to be ready in time?' asked Cherry.

'Yes,' answered one of the twins. 'I'm supposed to be collecting them next week. I need money in from everyone by Monday.'

'OK,' said Annie. 'Is that understood?'

'At least that solves the problem of outfits for the tap number,' said Cherry.

'*West Side Story* is going to be easy too,' said Annie. 'Just T-shirts and jeans for the boys, flared skirts for the girls. Although some of the girls will have to be boys, won't they?'

This problem was quickly sorted out.

'Wouldn't it look better if each gang was in a particular colour?' Robbie suggested. 'Just the T-shirts I mean. Like, black for Jets, white for Sharks.'

A quick tally showed that everyone could manage the right colour shirt for their gang.

'Great,' said Annie. 'That was a really good idea.'

'Now for the Magic Toyshop,' said Cherry. 'This is definitely going to be difficult.'

'Not necessarily,' said Annie. 'We can improvise. We can't start making elaborate costumes.'

126

'But what about the clowns and the jack-in-the-box?' asked Cherry.

'Well, we can make clown hats and the box itself – perhaps at your house, Cherry?'

'Fine,' said Cherry.

'But for the main clown costumes – I thought borrowing your fathers' trousers and braces and a big white shirt would be fine.'

'You can do a lot with make-up,' added Pip.

'Exactly,' said Annie. 'And I was hoping the clockwork mice could all find brown or grey tops and leggings to wear. We'll make the tails and ears and some cardboard keys.'

The 'ducklings' agreed that they could all get hold of a mouse-coloured outfit.

'Any ideas for us?' asked one of the twins.

'Have you any matching clothes?' asked Annie. 'Or don't you go in for dressing alike?'

'We have got some things the same,' said the twins.

'Anything suitable for rag dolls, Kim?' asked Cherry.

'We've got puffy-sleeved white blouses the same,' said Kim.

'Then perhaps we could wear a printed skirt,' said Susie. 'They'd be different colours, though.'

'That wouldn't matter,' said Annie. 'Are you any good at sewing?'

'Not too bad. Why?'

'I thought perhaps you could each make a simple white apron,' said Annie. 'That would look nice.'

As time was running out for the rehearsal, Annie decided to postpone further discussion.

'We can sort out the principals' costumes later,' she said to Cherry and Pip.

They got down to some dancing at last. It wasn't until the very end that Annie realized how quiet Sam had been all lunch-time.

While the girls were packing up, he was still hanging around, even though Robbie had gone. Annie wondered if he wanted to talk.

'Anything the matter, Sam?' she asked.

'Er, no, not really,' Sam replied. 'I'm in no hurry to get to the next lesson, that's all. Actually, I think I've left something in the boys' changing rooms. I'll just fetch it.'

The three girls left the gym before Sam came out again, and made their way across the yard towards the main block. As they rounded the corner of the dining-hall, Annie nearly tripped over a large foot.

'Look where you're going!' said a familiar voice. It was Wayne, with Darren at his elbow.

The girls walked on, without replying.

'They're waiting for Sam,' Pip said when they were out of earshot. 'Oh, I wish we could do something.'

'It must be awful for him,' said Annie, 'but we just seem to make it worse.'

'Perhaps he'll wait in the gym until the bell's gone,' said Cherry. 'By then, those two should have gone to lessons.'

'Don't count on it,' said Annie. 'I've heard they

128

skive most of the time.'

The girls went to their first lesson, feeling anxious for their friend. Sam came in five minutes after the bell, looking dishevelled and unhappy.

Mrs Clanger wasn't pleased with him for being late, nor for his untidy appearance. But Sam gave her no inkling of what had really been happening. He just shrugged his shoulders in answer to her questions.

'Do you think we should tell her?' Annie whispered to her friends. 'They might really hurt him one of these days.'

'I don't think he'd ever forgive us if we did!' said Pip. 'He's very proud, you know.'

'Poor Sam,' whispered Cherry. 'He doesn't deserve this!'

The question of Sam remained on Annie's mind. When the club held their next meeting at Cherry's, she was pleased to see him looking a little more at ease. Wayne and Darren had obviously left him alone lately.

'We've got to sort out what you're going to wear as the magician,' she said to him.

'Well I don't want to wear tights,' Sam said, rather anxiously.

'Fine,' said Annie. She suddenly saw how brave he was to get up on stage and dance in front of the whole school, when there were characters like Wayne and Darren in the audience. 'I think the main thing is a huge, swirling cloak.'

'Where do I get a huge, swirling cloak from?'

asked Sam with a grin.

'I'll ask my mum,' said Annie. 'She's an ace dressmaker. And I know we've got a load of shiny purple material she bought ages ago from a shop that was closing down. She always said it would come in useful one day!'

'I suppose I can wear my white tutu for the Christmas angel?' suggested Cherry.

'That's right,' said Annie. 'All you'll need to make is a gold star on a band for your hair.'

'What about you, Annie?'

'I've got a Scottish costume from a display at my old dancing school. It still fits me, just.'

'That's lucky,' said Pip. 'But who's going to make me a teddy-bear suit?'

'I think we're going to have to hire something from the fancy-dress shop for you. We'll have a whip round, don't worry. You won't have to pay it all yourself.'

Pip flushed. 'No really, I can pay.'

'We'll all pay,' said Annie. 'It's just your costume's more difficult, that's all.'

Mrs Stevens brought in a fresh batch of flapjacks, and some juice.

'As they went down so well last time, I thought I'd better make some more!' she said.

Sam pounced on a flapjack, but then announced he had to leave a bit early, as it was his father's birthday and the family were having a small party for him.

It wasn't very many minutes before Annie and

130

Pip left the Vicarage and began the short walk to the bus-station. Although it was only just after five, it was nearly dark, and the street lamps had been lit.

As they passed an alley-way, Annie glanced down it and thought she saw a dark shadow on the ground, moving slightly.

'Wait,' she hissed, putting a hand on Pip's arm. 'It looks like a big animal.'

They stopped and listened, feeling rather alarmed. A groaning noise came from the figure.

'It's a person,' whispered Annie. 'We'd better go and look.'

'I'm frightened,' said Pip, but she followed Annie into the alley-way all the same.

When Annie's eyes had adjusted to the greater gloom, she saw with a start that the figure on the ground was Sam.

'Sam!' cried Pip, recognizing him at about the same instant.

The girls knelt down beside him. Sam managed a wonky grin, although tears mingled with blood were trickling down his dark cheeks. One of his eyes had puffed up and was nearly closed.

'Whatever's happened, Sam?' cried Annie.

'Wayne and Darren,' he moaned.

'You mean they followed you to Cherry's?' Pip said, incredulously.

'I'm calling the police,' said Annie, standing up. 'This is serious.'

'No, no, please don't,' begged Sam immediately,

tugging at Annie's hand. 'What good will it do, even if I can prove they did it? They'll still be around at school whatever happens. It would just make it worse, believe me.'

'But we've got to tell someone!' cried Annie. 'Mr Reynolds, Mrs Clanger, someone!'

'No, you don't understand,' groaned Sam. 'They'd take it out on me. They don't care what anyone says to them.'

'Surely someone can do *something*!' said Annie helplessly.

'I just have to stay out of their way as much as I can,' said Sam. 'That's all I can do.'

'But when they keep following you …' began Pip. 'Oh, Sam!'

'I've got to get to my dad's party,' he said, wiping his face with a hanky. 'Some state to go to a party in.'

'Come back to Cherry's first,' suggested Annie, helping him up. 'You can clean up there. You won't frighten your folks quite so much then.'

'But what about Cherry's mum and dad?' said Sam. 'You mustn't tell them. I'll say I fell over if they ask.'

Sam made the girls promise not to tell anyone but Cherry about what had happened before he would agree to go with them.

Cherry was horrified when she opened the door to them.

'Sh,' said Sam. 'No questions, right. I just want to clean myself up.'

She smuggled him into the cloakroom before her mother saw him, supplying him with cottonwool and antiseptic cream.

'Whatever's happened to him?' she asked Pip and Annie, when she'd left him to it.

'Wayne and Darren must have followed us,' said Pip, 'and waited for him on his way home. They jumped out at him, only just down the road.'

'We must tell someone!' said Cherry. 'They can't just go around beating him up like this!'

'He won't let us,' explained Annie. 'He says it would only make things worse.'

'Look, I really must dash,' said Pip. 'I don't want to miss my bus again.'

Annie and Cherry exchanged glances. They were still totally mystified by the amazing car that had come to collect Pip the last time she missed her bus.

'I'll wait for Sam then,' said Annie. 'He might be glad of company walking into town.'

Sam looked a little more presentable when he emerged from the cloakroom, but Annie imagined he would still have a lot of explaining to do when he reached home.

'Are you OK now?' she asked him as they arrived at his front gate, which was just across the road from the bus-station.

'I'll live,' he said, with a grin. 'Thanks, Annie. And don't forget – I fell over!'

Annie sighed. 'I wish I could persuade you to tell the police,' she said.

'No chance,' he said. He gave her a wave and let himself in through the front door.

Over the weekend the three girls got together after dance classes at Miss Rodelle's to make clown hats, mouse tails and other accessories. Annie's mum started making an enormous cloak and a magician's cap for Sam.

As Annie had guessed, she was glad to put the yards of purple material she had been storing in the attic to good use.

The hire of a teddy-bear suit was arranged for Pip and, most exciting of all, the Dance Club T-shirts arrived. The twins brought them round to Annie's on Sunday afternoon.

'They're fantastic!' said Annie. 'I'm sure everyone will love them!'

'The logo looks terrific, doesn't it,' said one of the twins (Annie suspected it was Kim).

'Yes,' said the other twin, with a toss of her blonde pony-tail. 'All our friends outside the club will be madly jealous!'

Annie couldn't wait to show the shirts off to the rest of the club, especially Sam, who had designed the logo in the first place. When Monday morning came round, she arranged an extra lunch-time meeting with Mrs Race.

Sam came to school with a black eye, but Annie didn't have chance to say much to him, other than tell him about the meeting that lunch-time.

Annie, Pip and Cherry gulped down their lunch

134

in order to be first at the gym. They spread the batch of T-shirts out on a table, for the club members to admire as they came in. As everyone started trying on the T-shirts, Maria and Zoë walked into the gym. Annie thought Maria looked rather smug.

'We've just seen Sam,' Maria said.

Annie looked at her watch. 'He's probably on his way over. What are you two doing here anyway?' she asked suspiciously.

Maria and Zoë laughed. 'Just dropped in to say hello,' said Maria.

Annie noticed Maria's eyes resting on the T-shirts and detected a flicker of interest.

'And goodbye,' said Zoë, giggling.

They started moving back across the gym to the door.

'Don't bother to wait for Sam,' called Maria. 'He's not coming.'

'What d'you mean …?' began Annie, but the two girls had already left the gym.

'Don't take any notice of her,' said Cherry. 'She's just out to cause trouble.'

Annie frowned. 'She may know something we don't.' She turned to Pip. 'Have you spoken to Sam today?'

'No,' said Pip. 'He's been avoiding me. But Robbie may have – he's just come in.'

The friends went across to ask Robbie if he'd seen Sam.

'Yes,' Robbie replied. 'And he said he couldn't

come to the club. He gave me this letter for you.'

Annie guessed what it would say even before she'd ripped open the envelope—

Dear Annie, Pip and Cherry,
I'm awful sorry to let you down like this, but I just can't go on coming to Dance Club. I need to lie low for a while at school, and not go to places where W and D know I'm at.
I hope you'll understand,
Sam

'Well, that's it,' said Annie, when she'd finished reading the letter. 'End of show!'

· 12 ·

The Real Culprits

Even the news that she'd gained her National silver medal couldn't rescue Annie from the deep gloom she'd fallen into since Sam had dropped out of the club. There was no way they could teach anyone else Sam's parts with the show only days away.

The girls couldn't feel cross with Sam, either, after the beating up he'd suffered at Wayne and Darren's hands. They made a point of seeking him out and telling him they didn't blame him at all.

Sam looked relieved. 'Thanks,' he said. 'And I'm really sorry.'

'It's not your fault,' said Annie.

'By the way,' said Sam, 'I left my dance gear in

the gym at the last meeting. Did you pick it up for me by any chance?'

The girls told him they hadn't seen it, and he went off to ask Mrs Race. When they saw him later on, he told them nothing had been handed in.

'Someone's nicked it,' he said.

'Who would do such a thing?' cried Cherry.

'Maria?' suggested Annie. 'She was fairly keen for Sam to drop out.'

'No, I don't think it would be Maria,' said Sam. 'It's much more likely to be Wayne and Darren.'

'We ought to look in their lockers,' said Annie. 'They probably wouldn't have taken it out of school. I mean, it's no use to them, is it?'

'No,' agreed Pip. 'They'd have taken it out of spite, I expect.'

'I don't want to break into their lockers,' said Sam. 'It's just too dangerous.'

'We'll help you,' said Annie. 'We're not going to let them get away with anything else. They've done quite enough already.'

'I'll find out when their form's having games today,' suggested Pip. 'That would be a good time to do it.'

'But how are we going to get into the lockers?' asked Cherry.

'I've never picked a lock before,' said Annie, 'but I'll try anything once. You're supposed to be able to do it with a hairpin.'

'A padlock, though?' Sam asked. He looked doubtful. 'Tell you what. I'll nip into the changing

138

room while they're at games. They should have their locker keys in their trouser pockets.'

'Great,' said Annie. 'Then that's settled. Let's meet at the end of lunch-hour and Pip can tell us when we can go ahead.'

At twenty-past one, Pip met them with the news that the boys in Wayne and Darren's class would be out on the football field from 2 o'clock until 2.45.

'What lesson are we in then?' asked Cherry.

'English with Mrs Clanger,' said Pip. 'She'd certainly notice all four of us missing.'

'We'll have to think up some very convincing reason for going out of the classroom,' said Annie. 'In fact it would be better if we weren't all out together. Sam, if you could get out first to get the keys and pass them to me – I could do the next bit.'

'I want to come with you,' said Cherry.

'All right,' said Annie. 'But what excuse can we think of for getting out of English?'

'You're a good actress,' said Cherry. 'How about you're feeling really sick and I offer to go with you to the loo?'

'Perfect,' said Annie.

'I could say I wanted to go to the toilet,' said Sam. 'It won't take me long to run to the gym.'

'Perfect,' said Annie. 'But be careful not to get caught by another teacher, or you'll be in trouble.'

At five minutes past two, Sam asked to be excused. Annie was amazed at how quickly he was back. They had deliberately sat close to each other, so it was easy for him to pass the set of keys under the table.

'They're Wayne's,' whispered Sam. 'Darren didn't have any keys in his pocket. Good luck!'

A few minutes later, Annie went into action.

'Ooh!' she moaned loudly. 'Aaaagh!'

'Whatever's the matter?' asked Mrs Clanger, rushing over to her desk. Annie struggled to her feet and promptly doubled over, clutching her stomach.

'Gonna be sick!' Annie gasped.

'Shall I take her to the loo?' offered Cherry, her arm round her friend.

'Yes, yes, quick as you can,' said Mrs Clanger, ushering the pair out of the classroom door. 'And take her on to the sick-room, please, Cherry.'

Annie kept up the pretence along the corridors, in case another member of staff asked them what they were doing out of the classroom. Fortunately the sick-room was in the general direction of the locker-room. There was no one about. The locker-room was normally deserted in lesson-time.

Annie peeped round the door first, to make quite sure.

'It's OK,' she whispered to Cherry. 'Come on!'

They crept in, feeling like burglars themselves. Cherry quickly located Wayne's locker.

'Well done,' Annie whispered. They opened the locker and rummaged through it. At first it just seemed to be full of school books and Wayne's belongings but at the very back was a carrier bag which contained Sam's jazz shoes and leggings, and also, to their surprise, the spare pair of tap shoes that had gone missing.

'Got them!' cried Annie. 'At least we can get the stuff back to Sam. I don't suppose he'll let us report Wayne, though.'

'We can't really tell Mr Reynolds we sneaked off with Wayne's keys and looked through his locker, anyway,' Cherry giggled.

Annie was looking thoughtful. 'If Wayne had Sam's tap shoes – they probably would fit Darren – he's not that big … ' she mused, almost to herself.

'What are you getting at, Annie?'

'I mean Darren made the footprint in the clay and used the tap shoes so that Sam and the Dance Club would be suspected,' said Annie.

'But how are we going to tell anyone what we've found?' wailed Cherry.

But Annie was searching in the locker again.

'Wait a minute,' she said, 'what's this?'

She pulled out a floppy disk from under Wayne's books.

'Looks familiar,' Annie said, turning it over. 'Though the label's been torn off.'

Cherry laughed. 'How can a disk look familiar?' she said.

'Here,' said Annie. 'The last disk I backed up my project on had these white marks on it. I remember them clearly.'

Cherry and Annie looked at each other.

'If it *is* the same one,' Cherry said slowly, 'that

would clinch it.'

'Yes!' cried Annie. 'We must run it on the computer and find out for sure!'

The girls had to wait for their IT lesson later in the afternoon for the opportunity to do this. Sam was pleased to have his gear back and he and Pip were intrigued by Annie's theory about the disk. The four friends stood around Annie's computer while she tested the disk on it. On to the screen, sure enough, came the title of Annie's project, her name and form.

'I knew it!' said Annie. Her eyes were sparkling with excitement.

'What do we do now?' asked Cherry.

'Go straight to Mr Reynolds,' said Annie.

'But we can't tell him … ' Cherry began.

'I don't care if we get into trouble,' said Annie firmly. 'This is too important to keep to ourselves.'

'Just try and keep me out of it,' Sam pleaded.

'I'll do my best,' said Annie.

'I'll come with you,' said Cherry.

When the two girls explained they had found Annie's disk and Sam's tap shoes in Wayne's locker, the expression on Mr Reynold's face changed from one of suspicion to one of surprise.

'Are you quite sure about this?' he asked.

The girls nodded.

'Well I'm sure the police will find this very interesting,' he said. 'But Wayne! I know he's a bit silly sometimes, but getting caught up in a burglary … ' he shook his head, his brow furrowed.

Annie longed to tell him about the bullying, but knew she couldn't break her promise to Sam.

'Mind you,' said the headteacher, 'we mustn't go jumping to conclusions. And I must impress upon you, this *must* remain completely confidential for the time being.'

'Could I make a suggestion?' said Annie.

Mr Reynolds had moved over to the window and was staring out of it.

'Er ... yes. What is it, Annie?' he said, turning again to face them.

'It might be a good idea to search Darren's locker too – they go everywhere together.'

Mr Reynolds looked thoughtful. 'Yes, I'll do that. Just one question before you go ... how and why did you go into Wayne's locker in the first place?'

Annie came out of Mr Reynold's office with her ears burning.

'I hate telling fibs,' she said.

'Do you think he believed that you got your locker mixed up with Wayne's and your key just happened to fit his padlock?' asked Cherry.

'Shouldn't think so,' said Annie with a grin. 'But given we've probably solved the burglary, I don't think he'll be questioning us too closely, do you?'

'I hope you're right,' said Cherry.

'You'll see,' said Annie.

Annie's prediction was correct. Before school ended, she saw a police car draw up in the car park. A message came for Annie and Cherry to go to the headteacher's office.

PC Whiting was there when they walked in.

'As you have been so involved in uncovering the evidence, I thought you would like to know the outcome of the police investigation,' Mr Reynolds said.

'Yes,' said PC Whiting, smiling broadly at the girls. 'thanks to your find today, we have arrested two suspects.'

Annie looked at Mr Reynolds.

'Wayne and Darren,' Mr Reynolds said with a sigh. 'Some of the computer games were found in Darren's locker.'

'And the computer and printer were in the shed at the bottom of Darren's garden,' the officer added.

Annie felt immeasurable relief at the news. She grinned at Cherry.

'Apparently, Darren's family couldn't afford to buy him a computer,' said PC Whiting. 'He was desperate to have one of his own – he's pretty good with them, so his teacher said.'

'Yes, he has quite a talent in that direction,' said Mr Reynolds. 'Such a pity that he decided to resort to dishonesty. And Wayne's no great thinker, I'm afraid. Very easily led.'

Annie felt suddenly ashamed at her pleasure in catching the culprits. Bad as they were, she didn't like to think of the older boys going to prison. And she felt a twinge of sympathy for Darren, not being able to afford something he longed for. It would be like not being able to have ballet lessons.

'What will happen to them?' asked Cherry, who was obviously thinking along the same lines.

'Although it's serious, it's their first offence,' said PC Whiting, 'they'll very likely be let off with a caution. Then it's up to them.'

'They will be suspended immediately and permanently from Bishops, however,' said Mr Reynolds. 'Thieving cannot be tolerated here and it will be better for them to make a fresh start elsewhere.'

These replies made Annie feel much happier – firstly for Wayne and Darren, and secondly for Sam. He'd not have to face his tormentors again.

'Before you girls go back to your lesson,' said Mr Reynolds, 'I'd like to add my thanks to the constable's. And as a token of gratitude, I shall be allowing the Dance Club to run after all.'

'Oh thank you,' Annie cried, echoed by Cherry.

'By the way,' said the headteacher. 'Mr Farr and I would very much like to watch your dress rehearsal!'

Annie and Cherry left the office with lighter hearts than they'd had for weeks and rushed off to tell their friends the good news. There was no doubt in Annie's mind that the show would now go ahead. Her head was already racing with the last-minute rehearsals and finishing touches to the costumes that she'd have to arrange.

One of the big surprises of the week was that Maria and Zoë asked to rejoin the club. Annie and her friends were feeling so elated that they agreed, especially as Maria seemed apologetic.

'It'll be lovely to have the Spanish solo back in my ballet,' said Annie, beaming at them.

'And a good singer for 'Somewhere', I should think,' said Maria.

Annie looked at her. 'No,' she said. 'It's too late to swap back now.'

'But … ' Maria began.

'There's no question about it,' said Annie, determined to stick to her guns. 'Pip keeps the part.'

To her surprise, Maria said no more and accepted her decision.

'What d'you make of that?' asked Cherry later, when the friends were by themselves.

'A bit of a shock,' said Annie.

'I'm glad I didn't lose my part again,' said Pip looking pleased as Punch.

'I guess they just didn't want to miss out when they saw the club *and* the show were going ahead,' said Cherry.

'And the T-shirts,' said Annie. 'I could see Maria was dying to have one!'

The next few days were terribly busy in the buildup to Friday evening's concert. The dress rehearsal was to take place after school on Thursday. Annie and her friends grew terribly nervous, knowing that Mr Reynolds, Mr Farr, their music teacher, and Mrs Race would all be watching.

It was pretty chaotic, as dress rehearsals usually

are. At least they had no scenery or backdrops to shift. The worst technical problems they had to tackle were a couple of nippy costume changes and, of course, the recorded music.

Robbie had roped in one of his friends to work the tape recorder, but as he hadn't seen the dances before, and didn't know the music, there were several false starts and stops before the rehearsal was over. This made the dancers more nervous than ever and made the whole thing look very bitty. Annie just hoped he'd have the hang of it by the next day, but feared otherwise.

Another disaster was Pip's teddy-bear costume which Mrs Race had picked up for them from the fancy-dress shop. It was a couple of sizes too small, and when Pip joined in the energetic finale of the Magic Toyshop, the back seam split from waist to bottom.

'I'm sorry,' Pip wailed.

'Don't worry,' said Annie. 'Mum can mend it tonight. It's only the seam.'

Mrs Race and Mr Farr came to see them backstage. 'The headteacher had to rush off,' Mrs Race explained, 'but he asked me to wish you luck for tomorrow's performance.'

'We need it!' said Annie.

'I'm sure it will be all right on the night,' said Mr Farr. 'There are some very good numbers in the show. I'll keep an eye on your music man – see there aren't any hitches.'

'Oh thank you, Mr Farr!' cried Annie, feeling

very relieved.

Annie found herself left with lots of last minute repairs that evening. Apart from Pip's ripped teddy-bear costume, the jack-in-the-box's box had started to tear and several mouse ears had become detached from their headbands.

'What did you do with yourself before the Dance Club?' her mum teased her, as they sat sewing together.

'I can't really remember,' said Annie, 'but I do know it's helped me enormously to settle into Shropshire. I've hardly thought about Scotland at all these last few weeks.'

'I shouldn't think you've had time,' said her mum. 'Anyway, I'm pleased you're happy. It's great how a hobby like dancing or music helps you make new friends.'

'Oh, I can't believe it's the show tomorrow,' said Annie, her tummy suddenly tightening up. 'I just hope everyone remembers what they're supposed to be doing!'

Annie spent the whole of the next day worrying. At last seven o'clock came round. The first half of the concert consisted mainly of items from the school orchestra and the concert band. Annie, Cherry, Pip and Maria appeared in the choir at the very end. As usual, Maria sang a solo. Annie thought to herself once again that her voice, though powerful, was not half so tuneful as Pip's.

At the interval, the friends ran to the classroom which served as the girls' changing room. They threw on their costumes for the Magic Toyshop, yelling frantic last-minute instructions to the rest of the cast, most of whom were already costumed and made-up.

Sam and Robbie peeped round the door when the interval was nearly over. They seemed in high spirits.

'I'm really looking forward to this!' Sam said to them. 'Good luck, everyone!'

'Good luck!' the girls called back.

And then they were all in the wings of the school hall stage, listening to the opening bars of the music for their ballet. Annie whispered *good luck* to the 'ducklings' as they trooped past – the jack-in-the-box and the clockwork mice were first on stage. Then came the magician, the tumblers and clowns. Annie watched them all in a sort of agony, seeing her ideas, her movements finally come to life and willing each one of the dancers not to make a mistake. Sam was a superb magician, swooping around the stage in his swirling cloak.

Maria was the first soloist. Her Spanish dance was greeted with enthusiastic applause. Although Annie still felt quite cross with her, she had to admit she was an excellent performer.

'Ooh, it's me next,' whispered Cherry, coming up behind her in her white tutu.

'You'll be fine,' said Annie. She watched as her friend did the classical solo with great assurance. She knew Cherry would have preferred something livelier, but that hadn't stopped her dancing her best. Pip followed Cherry. It made Annie smile watching her do her forward bends very gingerly indeed. She didn't want to split her teddy-bear suit again!

After Pip's short comic dance, which produced laughter from the children in the audience, Annie stepped on stage for her own solo. She felt proud of the Macdonald tartan in her costume, as she began the Scottish dance which had already won her a silver medal.

She felt, rather than saw, an ocean of faces looking at her, but very quickly she forgot them all, forgot everything except the music and the dance. As her limbs moved in perfect harmony with the Scottish air, she forgot even that she was Annie Macdonald.

Everything after that went by in a dream. She only knew by the applause at the end of each item that it had been a success. She was on stage again for the Magic Toyshop finale, which was fast and furious. As it reached its climax, there was a tearing noise to her right. She looked across and saw Pip clutching the seat of her costume, and looking rather pink. Annie managed to move over and dance in front of her, to spare her further embarrassment.

Pip was first off stage. 'Thanks!' she called to Annie as Annie followed her off.

There was a lightning costume change, before the principal dancers could get back on stage for their tap number, sporting their new T-shirts.

Sam and Pip's duet followed. The warmth and loveliness of their singing reached the hearts of everyone who listened.

And then, almost in the wink of an eye it seemed, Annie was taking part in the club's finale – the Jets and Sharks dance from *West Side Story*. The audience loved it. There was a roar of applause as they struck their final tableau.

Robbie's friend forgot to pull the curtains across but it didn't matter. The show had been a success! The friends trooped backstage, congratulating one another.

'Thanks everyone!' said Annie. 'It was fantastic! You were all great!'

'Our very first show!' Cherry exclaimed.

'I wonder if there'll be any more for the Dance Club?' said Pip.

'Of course there will be,' cried Annie. 'This is just the beginning!'